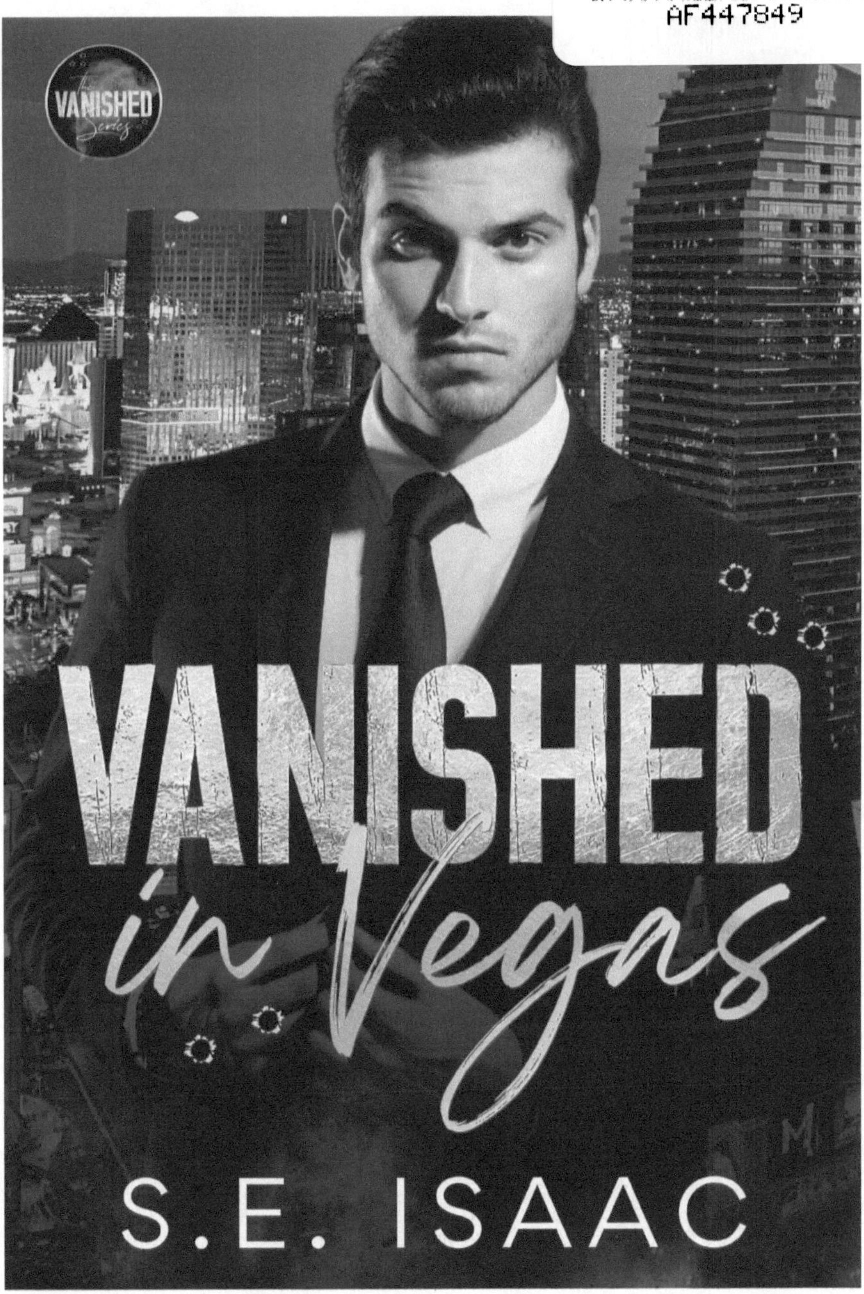
The
VANISHED
Series
VANISHED
in Vegas
S.E. ISAAC

Ebook Cover Designer: Matilda Martel
Paperback Cover Designer: Matilda Martel & S.E. Isaac

BLURB

Sofia Romano has just been flown to Las Vegas via her father's orders. She protested and demanded to stay in New York City; however, as always, her father won. Now, she's bound for living with her grimy, sleazeball of an uncle-- Uncle Tino. The man she despises most but just like everything else in her life, she doesn't have a say in the world.

Antonio Berlusconi owns Las Vegas. There isn't a single thing that happens in his city that he doesn't know about. That's how he knows the rat, Tino Romano just had a special delivery. A niece. And she's the perfect leverage to use against Tino by kidnapping her and making Tino sign over his rights to the biggest casino in Vegas. Simple enough. Right?

Just one problem, what do you do when the leverage is a green-eyed spitfire, who you crave like there's no tomorrow and couldn't harm a hair on her head even if you tried? You make her yours at any and all cost.

CHAPTER ONE

SOFIA

"It's a wedding for fuck's sake, Adrianna!" Rosaline-- Rose-- my baby sister shouted from the doorway. She stomped her foot in frustration.

"Just because it's a wedding doesn't mean we are no longer Romanos, Rosaline," Adrianna, my older sister, said firmly. Her gaze was locked on Rose. The tension in my room thickened, instantly.

"Sofia, tell Adrianna she doesn't need to bring a gun!" Rose pouted. They both turned their attention to me.

Being the middle sister, I always found myself in the middle of their issues. Today was no different. We were, in Miami, about to attend the wedding of the year. Rocco Levi was finally settling down and marrying Carrabelle Montagne. I didn't know either of them personally and honestly didn't care if I had stayed home or gone to the wedding.

My father had received an invitation to the wedding. He didn't like leaving New Jersey so he planned on sending money, flowers, and a card in his place. When Rose caught wind of his plan, she begged him to let her go instead. He of course said *no.* That's when she poured on her daddy's little girl charm.

There weren't many things my father would cave to; however, my sisters and I were occasionally one of those things. Two days later, the man gave in but gave his stipulations. Rose could go to Miami if Adrianna and I went with her, along with his goons. So... big sisters to the rescue.

Now, here we were in Miami, at some house my father

rented out for our two-day trips. Moments before, Rose busted in like the *Kool-Aid Man* and started bitching, Adrianna and I were discussing the weird feelings we were having about the wedding. I had woken up to a wave of emotions. They made my blood run cold. I wanted to bail. Adrianna did too.

The Levi's were bad news in my book. They had a history of blood-shed. Ten years ago, they had slaughtered an entire family. Thoughtlessly.

"Sofia already put her gun in her purse," Adrianna smirked, crossing her arms in front of her chest.

"Oh, for crying out loud," Rose groaned.

"Sorry, Rose," I offered her an apologetic smile. She glared at me, making me shrug and laugh. "Better safe than sorry."

"It's. A. Wedding," Rose said slowly and dramatically. Adrianna and I exchanged glances and rolled our eyes. "But whatever. Bring a gun. What do I care? Dad is already sending his meatheads to babysit us. We all know they'll be packing heat. Why don't we just slap neon lights on our asses so we really draw everyone's fucking attention to us?"

"You're being such a diva, Rosaline," Adrianna growled.

"Fuck you," Rose huffed.

"You better mind your fucking tone with me or I'll see to it that none of us go, Rosaline Romano."

"You're such a bitch!" Rose sobbed, storming out of the room.

"Adrianna," I groaned, "really?"

"What?" Adrianna shrugged then gestured for me to zip the back of her dress.

"She's not like us," I replied, zipping up her dress. She spun around, showing off her beautiful light blue dress. She smiled brightly.

"You think I don't know she isn't like us?" Adrianna asked, facing me.

"Then can't you be more sensitive with her?"

"She can toughen up." Adrianna shrugged thoughtlessly.

"We did this to her," I reminded her.

It was the truth. Rose was more sensitive than Adrianna and me. We've busted our asses to shelter her from certain things that come with being a Romano. Life as a caproregime's daughter wasn't a walk in the park. There were so many rules, dos and don't dos. Eyes were always on us. And, our lives were always in jeopardy.

Even though we were close in age-- 20, 19, and 18-- Adrianna and I protected Rose from the dark side of life. If we even caught wind that someone might be thinking of looking at her the wrong way, we handled it. If she got in trouble with our parents, Adrianna and I took the physical punishment on her behalf. We went through hell so she could walk amongst flowers with her head in the clouds. It's what we did as her big sisters.

"Well, we need to *undo* this," Adrianna sighed, bringing me back to reality. "Immediately."

"We can't just wave our fingers and magically undo all of it, Adrianna," I groaned.

"Yeah, well, what's she going to do when dad sends us off?" Adrianna crossed her arms in front of her chest.

"What? Why would he send us off?"

Adrianna glances at the open door then back at me. I nodded in understanding. One of our dad's goons was probably listening at the door.

"Nosey fucker!" I yelled in the direction of the door. Adrianna laughed and grabbed her purse.

"Let's go find Rose then we can get this show on the road," she said, still laughing.

"Sounds like a plan." I grabbed my purse then linked arms with her as we walked out of my room and down the hallway towards Rose's room.

"Rose will still go off to the university and join E.C.M.P. Right?" I whispered into Adrianna's ear.

"No. And this will probably be the last event we go to for a while," she admitted. There was a look of sadness in her eyes. It wasn't like Adrianna to show weakness. She was the toughest out of the three of us. Seeing her vulnerable made my stomach knot and struck fear into my soul.

What the hell was going on?

CHAPTER TWO

"Why the fuck am I even going to this mother fucker's wedding?" I growled, stepping out of the car. Howard closed my door and stood a few steps ahead of me.

Howard was the youngest of the crew. Twenty or twenty-one. Didn't care enough to ask. I just knew he looked wet behind the ears. Niccolai, my underboss, had picked him and asked to bring him into the crew. I trusted Niccolai with my life; therefore, I gave the kid a chance. As long as Howard worked hard to do as I said and stayed the hell out of my way, he and I would get along just fine.

"You said you wanted to show your face, while we were here in Miami, Boss," Eddie reminded me, chuckling. I glanced at him. He was standing on the sidewalk, waiting for me. He smirked and shrugged slightly.

Eddie was my cousin, on my mom's side. We grew up together. He was like a brother to me. When I took over the head of the table for our family, it was made sense that he run one of my caproregimes.

"Thank God I'll be far away from this hellhole and back in *my* city." I stepped onto the sidewalk next to Eddie.

"Still complaining about this wedding, I see," Niccolai laughed, walking up behind us.

"Fuck you, Niccolai," I laughed.

Niccolai and Eddie both chuckled. The other guys who came with us, stuck to what they did best. They kept their eyes on everything around us. Prepared to do whatever it took at any given moment.

"After you, Boss," Eddie gestured for me to walk ahead.

"Maybe I want you to go first just in case someone shoots up the place," I retorted. Eddie's eyes searched mine, no doubt looking for a glimpse of humor in them.

When you're the head of the family, it is hard to crack jokes. Everyone always wants to take my words seriously. Not that I blame them. Going against any of my orders would be hell to pay.

"I'm kidding, Eddie. Fuck," I growled, walking ahead of him.

"Sorry, Boss," Niccolai called out behind me. I waved off his words and headed towards the front of the church. Harold and Flint ran ahead of me, clearing my path. Niccolai and Eddie caught up to me. Niccolai walked to my right. Eddie walked a few steps behind me with the rest of the crew behind him.

We passed by several groups of men standing around outside, who were smoking. They were dressed in expensive suits and designer shoes. Men with or from money. They all eyed me as I walked by but didn't utter a word. If they had, one of my guys would have popped off at the mouth.

A smug grin tugged at the corners of my mouth. It was a majestic feeling to know the power I held in my hands. To know that I didn't need to ever lift a finger. I had guys that would take care of my light and dirty work.

"Whoa. Who are they?" Eddie's words had me stopping in my tracks.

I turned to see where he was looking. The guys parted like the sea, allowing me a view of the three women they were staring at. They were standing next to a black *Escalade* with men in suits posted around them. All three of the women were beautiful, but the one in the pink dress had my attention. My full attention.

"Yes. Who are they? The one in the pink specifically," I said, looking the woman over.

She appeared to be in her early twenties. A bit young

for my usual taste, considering I was thirty-two, but there was something about her. Her dark brown hair was pinned up. She wore pink-jeweled earrings that matched her dress and heels. Her make-up surprised me. It looked like she barely wore any. Generally, women who came to these big events wore make-up like a damn clown. But not this woman.

I glanced at the other two women. They weren't painted with make-up either.

"I recognize one of the guys next to them, Boss," Maxwell said. "The guy to the far right works for Mario Romano. The three girls are probably Mario's daughters."

"Who would have known Mario, could help create three beauties," Niccolai laughed.

Mario Romano was a ruthless, heartless, piece of shit. He operated out of New Jersey under the De Santos Family. I had never met him, but the stories I had heard about him were enough for me to despise him.

"I want her name by the time we leave here," I said, looking at the woman in pink again. As though she had sensed me looking, her eyes crossed the parking lot and met my gaze. She smiled.

"I'm willing to bet, she'd be up for a conversation with you, Boss," Eddie glanced at me and grinned.

"Isn't it tacky to hit on a woman at a wedding?" I asked, shaking my head.

The thought of walking over to some random woman at a wedding and telling her I thought she was beautiful reminded me of the cheesy movies my sister gushed about. Did women really like that shit? To me, it was creepy and would earn me a well-deserved *Get lost, Creep!*

CHAPTER THREE

SOFIA

"Ooo. Sofia, he's hot," Rose gushed, staring at the mystery man, who I had just spotted.

"He is pretty yummy, huh?" I laughed.

"Go get his number!" She pushed me in his direction. I stumbled forward. Lenny and Case--my dad's hired muscles-- grabbed me and held me upright.

"Thanks, boys," I smiled then turned a glare on Rose. She smiled innocently.

"My bad, Sofia."

"Don't make her look desperate, Rose," Adrianna groaned. "Sofia can have any bozo here. She doesn't need you throwing her at men."

"Was just trying to help," Rose grumped, crossing her arms in front of her chest. "You need to get laid, Adrianna. You're bitchy lately."

The goons guarding us looked humorously mortified by Rose's words. They looked everywhere but at us. Not that I blamed them. Adrianna was a hothead. If they looked at her the wrong way, she'd drop kick them and have them eating curb.

"Rosaline, unless you want me to make a scene here, I suggest you keep your mouth shut. Understood?" Adrianna growled.

"Fine," Rose nodded. She held up her hands in surrender and took a few steps away from Adrianna.

"Smart move," Adrianna replied coldly.

"Let's just go inside," I offered, hoping to bring peace to the two of them.

"Agreed. Let's go." Adrianna said, linking her arm with mine. She looked at Rose, who stood frozen in place. "Come on, brat. Can't leave you out here."

"You're the sweetest," Rose giggled then linked arms with Adrianna on the opposite side of me. "But we really should get you on meds or something."

This time I laughed. Rose was a glutton for punishment. It was like she had a death wish or something. If she kept barking up this tree, Adrianna would grant her wish.

"I love you, guys," Rose laughed.

"Love you too, Rosaline," I smiled. We both looked at Adrianna. Rose gave Adrianna puppy-dog eyes. Adrianna rolled her eyes.

"Come on. You know she won't stop until you say it back." I playfully bumped Adrianna with my hip. "You know you want to."

"Adrianna," Rose stuck out her bottom lip and fluttered her eyelashes.

"Oh. Jesus. I love you. Now, stop that," Adrianna busted out laughing. "Let's get you, two hooligans, inside."

We walked across the parking lot in the direction of Mr. Sexy-Pants and his entourage. My heart raced with each step I took. The heat in my cheeks rose. I didn't remember the last time I blushed over a guy.

"Incoming," Adrianna whispered teasingly as we stepped onto the sidewalk.

Mr. Sexy-pants gestured for the other men to step to the side, which they quickly did without hesitation. He stepped out of our way, but his eyes remained on me. I felt like a gazelle about to be pounced on by a cheetah. A very sexy cheetah.

"If you're going to eye-fuck my sister, you should at least say *hello* first," Adrianna said, bringing us to a halt in front of Mr. Sexy-

Pants. Thankfully, he didn't find her unlady-like words threatening and instead laughed.

He stepped in front of us, acknowledged my sisters then looked down at me. He smiled a smile that made me want to strip him of every article of clothing and have my way with him. Damn, he was sexy.

"I was going to wait until after the wedding to approach you," he chuckled, extending his hand out to me. "I'm Antonio Berlusconi."

"Sofia Romano," I said, trying to keep my tongue in my mouth. I placed my hand in his, expecting a handshake. To my surprise and schoolgirl delight, he brought my hand up to his lips and kissed it softly.

"It is a pleasure to make your acquaintance, Miss Romano." My name rolled off his tongue so smoothly that it made my knees go weak.

"Likewise, Mr. Berlusconi."

One of my dad's guards cleared their throat. An indication that Antonio had been holding my hand for far too long. I rolled my eyes and glared at the goon.

"It's my hand. Relax," I stated firmly.

"Just doing my job, Signorina Romano," Kit replied.

"I'm pretty sure our father didn't say no touching a boy's hand, Kit," Adrianna replied coldly.

"No, Signorina Romano. He said no touching any part of a...," Kit looked at Antonio, "...boy."

Antonio's jaw tightened. A vein in his neck pulsed. He said nothing; however, if looks could kill, Kit would have fallen over dead.

I turned to Kit.

"Kit, apologize to Mr. Berlusconi," I snapped, in Antonio's defense. Kit's eyes widened. "Now!"

Kit looked at Antonio. His nostrils flared as he took deep breaths.

"My apologies, Mr. Berlusconi," Kit said.

Antonio ignored Kit completely and looked at me.

"Save me a dance at the reception?" he grinned slyly.

"Definitely," I smiled.

He kissed my hand once more. This time his eyes were locked on Kit. A smirk plastered across his face. He was daring Kit to say something and I was eating it up. I loved a bad boy.

"See you later, Miss Romano." He slowly released my hand, never breaking eye contact with me. "Ladies," he smiled at Adrianna then Rose.

"Mr. Berlusconi," they said in unison. He chuckled and stepped aside allowing us to pass by.

"He totally wants to bone you," Rose giggled as we continued down the sidewalk.

"Yeah, he does," Adrianna laughed. "Maybe he'll kidnap you afterward and you'll finally have some fun."

"If he does, don't come looking for me," I grinned.

***

We signed the guest book then made our way farther inside the church to find our seats. The church was just like our Catholic church back home. Grand and elegant. Not a penny went to waste.

"Bride side, right?" Rose whispered. We looked around at those already seated in the pews.

"That's what dad said," I replied, ushering her into a pew towards the middle of the bride's side.

I sat between her and Adrianna. Kit and the guys stood in the aisle, waiting for us to scoot over and make room for them.

"Not happening. We'll be fine," Adrianna said. "Go sit in the back."

"Your father told us to--" Kale replied.

"This is God's house so you're off duty for now," I smiled. They looked at each other but didn't move.

"You're making a scene," Rose growled in a hushed tone. "Go find a seat somewhere."

"Agreed. We'll be right here if you need us," I said, gesturing at the back of the church.

They opened their mouths to say something but closed them just as fast. Kit gestured with his head for them to go to the back. They exchanged glances once more and then walked off.

"Drives me nuts," Adrianna muttered.

"Ditto," Rose sighed.

I looked around the room. There were so many familiar faces. Some were good news. Others, not so much. Hopefully, they'd behave themselves. Would hate to see a woman's beautiful day ruined.

"Look, Kimberly Russo and Carla De Santos are both here," I said, pointing at first Steffani then Chiara.

They both must have sensed us talking about them because they looked back at me as I pointed. I waved at both of them. They waved back before turning their attention back to those they were with.

"After this, we'll go say hello to them. Father will throw a fit if we don't acknowledge Uberto's kid," Adrianna whispered.

She was right. Carla was Uberto De Santos' daughter. And Uberto was the Boss, our father worked under. Greetings weren't always pleasantries. Sometimes it was strictly politics; however, we were in the same sorority and friends.

"Or we could say hello because she's my friend," I replied.

"Friends?" Adrianna rolled her eyes.

"Yes," I nodded. "Friends."

CHAPTER FOUR

ANTONIO

The bride had finally made her way down the aisle and the show was on the road, but fuck, this was boring. The only thing keeping me from leaving was Sofia. Before the wedding had started, I had found a seat on the groom's side, two rows back from where she was sitting on the bride's side. It was a bit stalkerish for me but I couldn't help myself.

"Stare any harder at her and you're going to put a hole through her, Boss," Eddie said softly, leaning closer to me. There was amusement in his tone.

"Fuck you," I muttered. He shrugged his shoulders and chuckled. "Next time, you aren't coming with me."

"Ah. Come on, Boss. Can't leave the kid at home," Niccolai joked quietly to the other side of me.

"Yeah, Boss. Can't leave *the kid* at home," Eddie mocked softly, making Niccolai and I laugh.

"She's definitely interested in you, Boss. Look," Niccolai nudged me slightly with his elbow.

I looked where he was staring and my eyes landed on Sophia. When our eyes met, she blushed then quickly faced forward as though it never happened. It was such a childish gesture; however, I found myself smiling like an idiot.

"Never seen you smile so big, Boss," Niccolai whispered.

"Yeah. It's fucking weird, right, Niccolai?" Eddie said. An old lady sitting in front of us turned around and frowned.

"Language. We're in the Lord's house," she said in disgust.

"Mind your business, hag," Eddie grumped.

The woman's eyes narrowed in on him. Anger filled her eyes. She was ready to give him a piece of her mind.

"You–" she began. Eddie flashed open his suit jacket revealing his pistol that was holstered inside. Her eyes widened as the color drained from her face. She couldn't turn around fast enough.

"Really, Eddie?" I chuckled.

"She's just a nobody, Boss," he said, frowning at the back of the woman's head.

"Just try to be on your best behavior," I rolled my eyes. "And watch your mouth."

"You got it, Boss." He nodded as he leaned back into the pew.

"How long is this thing anyway? Shouldn't it have started by now?" I asked Niccolai.

"Want me to go see what's taking them so long, Boss?" Niccolai whispered. I shook my head and pulled out my phone.

"No. Don't bother," I swiped my phone on. "Check in with Petey. See how things are going with the Manny situation."

"I'm on it, Boss," he said, fishing his phone out of his pocket.

"Seventy-two hours. That's it," I said firmly.

"I'll let him know, Boss." He began to stand but I shook my head. I gestured at the priest, who was about to give the infamous line and the last thing we needed was Niccolai ruining this damn wedding.

"If there is anyone who objects please speak now or forever hold your peace," the priest spoke.

The doors of the church flew open. They crashed loudly against the walls. My crew swarmed around me protectively as we all turned our attention to the back of the church. Standing there was Timur Fedorov. Next to him were a few of his men, who had their weapons drawn.

This wedding was about to turn into a real shit show. There was bad blood between Timur and the Levi Family. Literally. Sylvester Levi had given the orders to have the entire Fedorov Family murdered. Yet somehow Timur made it out alive.

"Time to go," I whispered.

"Boss?" Niccolai and Eddie said in unison.

"That's Timur Fedorov." I pointed at Timur as he walked by him and acknowledged him with a slight nod of my head. Doubtful that he noticed me since there was murder in his eyes.

"Let's get the boss out of here!" Eddie growled. They began to usher me towards a side door in the church. Their weapons aimed in all directions, waiting for the unexpected.

"Wait," I protested. For the first time in my life, I was worried about someone else's safety– Sofia's.

I looked over at her and my mouth gaped open. I expected to find her huddled down in the pew with the other two women. However, her response to the armed men surprised me.

Sofia stood in a defensive stance. A pistol was in her hand, aimed towards Timur as he walked to the front of the church. The oldest of the three women also had a weapon drawn and pointed towards the back of the church. She shouted something at the other two sisters. Sofia nodded while the youngest stared at Timur with wide eyes. Shellshocked perhaps? Sofia and the oldest each grabbed one of the girl's arms and pulled her from the pew.

Sofia's eyes were filled with intense rage. She went from being a beautiful and innocent woman to a passionate, fierce temptress. The type of woman who could burn down the entire world and not bat an eyelash. The kind of woman the devil would fear.

"So fucking sexy," I whispered with a slight chuckle.

"What? Boss, we gotta go," Eddie urged me towards the exit. I looked again for Sofia.

Her guards from outside surrounded her and the other two women. Half of the guards had their weapons drawn at the men at the front of the church. The other half were ushering Sofia and them out the side door. The moment Sofia disappeared out of view my nerves relaxed because now she was safe.

"Let's go," I ordered, walking calmly away from the pew towards the side door Flint had opened. His gun was also pointed at the guys at the front; however, he wouldn't shoot unless I ordered it or he felt my life was in imminent danger.

"Get the boss out of here!" Niccolai growled, jumping over several pews and making his way to us. "Now!"

"Chill, Niccolai. It's a hit. I don't think I made the list," I chuckled, walking out the door past Flint.

"Now's not the time to joke, Boss," he groaned. "We need to get you somewhere safe."

"We're out of the fucking church. Calm your fucking tits." I rolled my eyes.

He waved his arm as my black SUV came barrel-assing through the church grass over to us with Monty behind the wheel. He swerved the vehicle and I was damn near thrown in the back by Niccolai. He and I were going to have a long discussion about man-handling me. For now, I'd let him get away with it since he thought he was *saving me* from the *bad guys.* Mother fucker. We are the bad guys.

CHAPTER FIVE

SOFIA

"When we go in, keep your fucking mouth shut, Rosaline," Adrianna warned Rose, who was already in tears. We hadn't even faced our father yet and she was already bawling like a baby.

"Rose, get yourself together," I whispered, rubbing her back.

"Don't fucking baby her, Sofia. Now is not the time for weakness!" Adrianna snapped at me.

"Calm your fucking attitude. I'm not Rose, I'll fight your ass!" I growled back. Adrianna took a step closer to me. Our faces were now inches away from each other.

"I see someone wore their big girl panties today," she smirked. "Think you can take me, little Sofia?"

"If you don't get the fuck out of my face, you'll find out." My eyes were locked on hers. There was no way in hell I was backing down to her. I was tired of her shit.

When we got word that Sylvester Levi and his son Rocco, the groom, had been executed, Adrianna flipped out. She bitched how our father would never let us live this down. Then we were told that the bride had been kidnapped. Rose lost it. She cried hysterically, which added to Adrianna's annoyance. Adrianna went full bitch mode on Rose.

I snapped at Adrianna in Rose's defense. It only made matters worse for Rose and me because then on the three-hour flight, Adrianna raged on about how Rose was a big baby and I babied her. I didn't even bother responding to her. Talking to her when she was on one of her bitchy tangents was pointless. I'd have a better chance of getting a rock to respond to me.

The double doors to my father's conference room opened. Someone cleared their throat. Adrianna and I slowly took our eyes off each other. We looked into the room.

"Papa," my sisters and I said in unison.

"Come in," my father replied cooley, granting us access into the room. We quickly stepped inside and Al, who stood by the doors, shut them behind us.

Our father was sitting in his leather chair, at the head of the long table. His hands folded on top of the mahogany table. His large signet ruby diamond ring that he wore on his pinky finger gleamed in the lighting.

The table was filled by his soldiers. They were dressed in their fancy suits. Their eyes locked on my sisters and me.

"Cut it off," my father ordered.

My sisters and I quickly looked at him. He wasn't looking at us. He was staring at Joey, one of his slimiest goons. Joey had sat at the table for nearly two decades. However, his loyalty had recently been questioned.

"Boss?" Joey's voice trembled as he turned his attention to my dad.

"Prove your loyalty. Cut your finger off," my father replied coldly.

Oh no, I gasped internally. This was the last thing I wanted to witness. It wouldn't be my first time; however, who the fuck liked watching someone cut off a body part? My dad was a sick fuck.

"What?" Rose squeezed softly next to me. I kept my eyes on my dad but reached for her hand. When our fingers touched, she frantically grabbed my hand and squeezed it hard.

"Would you like us to leave, Papa?" Adrianna asked without

any signs of emotion in her tone.

"No," he replied flatly. His eyes locked firmly on Joey.

"Don't cry," Adrianna muttered under her breath. No doubt her words were meant for Rose.

Rose's hand trembled forcefully. I gripped her hand tighter, hoping to send her my strength and calm her nerves. This was the type of darkness Adrianna and I had worked hard to guard her against. We tried to let her see our father in a different light; however, this was who he was. A monster.

"I don't believe I stuttered. Did I stutter, Carlo?" my father asked, looking at Carlo, who sat to his right.

Carlo Russo was another piece of work. He and my father grew up together. They were the best of friends, who shared common interests like taking baseball bats to people's knees and making people swim with the fish.

"No. You didn't stutter, Boss," Carlo replied in his deep raspy voice. A lifetime of smoking had fucked his voicebox. Every time he talked, it made me cringe.

My father's goons stared at Joey. A ray of emotions etched on their faces. Some looked at him with sympathy-filled eyes, while others looked at him in disgust. My father's eyes however were locked on Joey like a hawk ready to destroy its prey.

"Do you not want to show your loyalty to me? Or perhaps you spit on the Romano name and the De Santos Family?" My father's words were cold as ice.

De Santos. Not a name to take lightly. If my father was bringing up their name then Joey had crossed more than just my father. De Santos was top of the food chain. The Boss. My father worked as his caporegime for an eternity. Joey's name being on De Santos's radar should put a fear of God into Joey. It was one thing to piss my father off. It was ten times worse to piss off De Santos.

"Never, Boss. My loyalty lies with you and the family," Joey blurted. "I've been loyal for years. I'm no rat. I swear!"

"Watch your tone," Carlo growled.

"Boss, I swear," Joey said, not even acknowledging Carlo's warning.

"Cut your fucking finger off to prove your loyalty before I have your fucking head cut off!" My father slammed his fists down onto the table. The table shook and the percussion echoed throughout the room. Several were startled in the room to include Rose, Adrianna, and me.

"For fuck's sake," I muttered under my breath. *Just let us fucking leave already.*

"Here," Carlo said, pushing a cigar cutter across the table to Joey.

Joey's face drained of color. His eyes widened and he swallowed hard. He stared at the cigar cutter then looked at my father and back at the cigar cutter. I could see the wheels turning from where I stood.

Joey was going through every option possible. One, he makes a break for the door. That'd end with him tackled by Al and probably a broken neck upon impact. Two, he begged my father for another way to prove his loyalty. That option would make the most sense to most; however, this was a mafia, not the *Girl's Scouts.* Joey trying to talk his way out of the situation would end in him being tortured for being *a rat.* The option with the least consequences would be him cutting his damn finger off. As fucked up as that sounded.

Adrianna and I glanced at each other. The look in her eye told me she was thinking of a way to get us out of the room. She didn't want any part of what was unfolding in front of us, either. If we were lucky, our mother would arrive home from wherever the hell she was. Our father didn't conduct the messy business when she was home. But the bastard had no problems showing the violence around his daughters. Just one more reason I hated him.

"Paulie, go get a tarp and machete," my father ordered, catching my attention.

"For crying out loud! It's just a fucking finger," Adrianna shouted with no hint of nerves.

She stormed over to Joey, snatched the cigar cutter off the table with one hand, and grabbed Joey's with her other hand. She slipped his finger into the cigar cutter. All eyes were on her, including my father who grinned.

"Wh… what are you doing?" Joey stammered, looking up at her. She looked down at him emotionlessly.

"It's just a finger," she muttered seconds before Joey cried out in pain.

Adrianna had squeezed the blade shut around Joey's finger. Sadly, she didn't have enough strength to cut his finger off so the blade struck the bone. Blood seeped out from under the metal. Tears filled Joey's eyes and silence filled the room.

"Finish it!" she demanded Joey, grabbing his other hand and placing it on the cigar cutter. "It's better than death."

Joey closed his eyes and nodded. A single tear slid down his cheek.

Snip, the sound the blades made as they struck each other and cut through the flesh and bone.

Joey cried out as his finger fell to the table. Blood sprayed from where his finger once was and the task was finally done. Or so he thought. I knew better.

Adrianna's rash decision to help him cut off his finger had just made things worse for him. She was a woman. Men were supposed to be stronger than us frail women; however, she had grown a pair and been the one to cut his finger first. The finger wouldn't be the last thing Joey would lose today. Because he'd undoubtedly lose his life next.

"My little girl has no fear," my father said, making the other men, except Joey, laugh. "Paulie?"

"Yeah, Boss?" Paulie asked.

"Handle this weak piece of shit." My dad's words came out

between clenched teeth. His eyes were narrowed in on Joey. Adrianna tensed but said nothing. She simply walked back over to Rose and me.

I wanted to scold her for ending Joey's life; however, I know she had acted on emotions and not logic. Adrianna was smarter than this. For her to act so impulsive, she must have something heavy weighing on her heart. Perhaps the wedding had gotten to her more. I thought she was just being a bitch to Rose and me, but the fact that maybe she was scared never crossed my mind.

I glanced over at Adrianna. Her jaw was clenched. The look in her eyes was emotionless. She had drifted off to a different place to battle her emotions. A method we had been taught at our *preparatory* school for.

"No!" Joey shouted as Paulie and Marcel grabbed him and yanked him out of his seat. The chair crashed to the floor as Joey tried to break free. "Boss, I swear! I'm no rat! I cut off my finger!"

"Get that piece of shit out of here...And make him suffer," my father added with a smirk.

"You got it, Boss," Marcel and Paulie replied.

Al opened the doors. Joey was dragged from the room, kicking, screaming, and begging for his life. His pleas fell onto deaf ears. Once my father made up his mind that was the end of the discussion.

"You girls will be leaving Jersey," my father said, grabbing my sisters and my attention.

"Leaving?" Rose asked.

"Yes. It isn't safe here, my flower," he replied before he opened his cigar box and pulled out a cigar. "Hand me my cigar."

Sick fuck, I thought. Only a psycho could use a cigar cutter that was just used to cut a man's finger off.

"Yours is dirty. You can use mine, Boss," Carlo offered, pulling his cutter out of his pocket. He swiftly clipped the end of my father's cigar. My father nodded his head in acknowledgment.

He placed the cigar in his mouth then flicked his lighter, sparking the end of his cigar. He inhaled sharply. The gesture of a cigar being lit always made my stomach knot. I hated cigars almost as much as I hated my father.

"We are leaving, Papa?" Adrianna asked, prompting the conversation. No doubt she wanted the conversation to hurry up so we could leave the room.

"Yes. It isn't safe here. Not after the shit that happened to the Levi Family," he shook his head.

"Will we be going to the university early?" she asked.

"No," he replied cooly, taking a puff of his cigar. "You will be going to stay with the Rossi's. Rose will go to Portland with the Tacchelli's."

"And Sofia?" Rose asked on my behalf.

I already knew where I was going. My stomach knotted and I fought the urge to rip my father's fucking head off.

"She will be going to Vegas to stay with your Uncle Tino," my dad replied.

"I can go to Vegas instead," Adrianna offered.

"I'll be fine," I stated. She and Rose looked at me. Rose looked terrified. Adrianna's eyes were emotionless; however, deep down I knew she was angry with my father's decision.

Our Uncle Tino was a druggy, sleazeball. Drugs and prostitutes were his thing. I had spent one summer there by myself, when I was twelve and almost ended up sold to a Cuban drug dealer for a shipment of cocaine. I never told my father because my father thought his little brother was the best thing next to sliced bread.

"Then it is settled." My father took another puff of his cigar and blew the smoke up into the air. "You'll pack your things, say goodbye to your mother and be on your way."

"As you wish... Papa," I replied. My icy stare set on him as I bowed my head slightly.

Rose and Adrianna would be safe under the protection of the Tacchelli's and Rossi's. I, on the other hand, would have to fear for my life. There was no way in hell I'd stay with my Uncle Tino and worry about being sold off for drugs, but arguing with my father was pointless. He wouldn't believe me that his brother was a piece of shit.

For now, I'd do as I was told, make my way to Vegas and then I'd vanish. I'd be safer on my own anyway.

CHAPTER SIX

ANTONIO

"Ear," I growled, sitting back in the chair.

"No! No! Please!" Manny screamed.

Manny Paloma ran a small crew under me. He did as he was told and kept his head down. Other than his weekly check-ins I didn't see him much. Didn't care to see him much more than that. As long as he followed the rules, he was fine to live his life as he deemed fit. In his case that involved booze, drugs, gambling, and laying low– Until a few days ago, while I was in Miami for the wedding. That's when the tables turned and Manny made my list.

"You got it, Boss," Flint replied. He grabbed a scalpel off the table then cut the flesh where Manny's ear and head met. Manny shouted out in pain. He bucked frantically in the chair he was bound to.

"Silence him. He's giving me a fucking headache," I muttered, pinching the bridge of my nose.

Eddie grabbed an oily rag off the floor and shoved it into Manny's mouth as Manny screamed again. Flint did a few more cuts until the ear was finally freed. He held out Manny's ear to me.

"I don't fucking want that," I frowned.

Flint and Eddie looked at each other and chuckled. Flint tossed the ear in the bucket of lye a few feet from him then looked at me for his next set of instructions.

"Manny, you did this to yourself," I smirked. Manny's eyebrow raised and he stared at me in confusion. "You thought I wouldn't know what was going on in my city? I own this city. There isn't a single thing that goes on in Vegas that I don't know about!"

He continued looking at me like an idiot.

"He thinks I'm an idiot." I gestured at myself. "Am I a fucking an idiot? Maybe I missed a memo or something?"

"No, Boss. You're no idiot," Eddie replied, smacking Manny in the back of the head hard.

"Yeah, you're no idiot, Boss," Flint nodded. "This piece of shit is the fucking idiot for underestimating you."

"Manny. Manny. Manny," I shook my head and tsked. "Did you really think I wouldn't do anything to you once I learned of your sex trafficking ring?"

His eyes widened, dread and pure terror turning them glossy He shook his head wildly, yelling something against the rag.

"Is that an apology?" I sneered. "Are you sorry for bringing that garbage to my city?

Manny nodded frantically. Again, he uttered words but they were jumbled by the rag. Not that hearing them would get him out of this situation. He and his crew had kidnapped, abused, and hurt women.

"My rule was simple. Never harm women or children. That's an easy one, right?"

"Too easy, Boss," Flint nodded.

"Life could have been good for you, Manny," I said standing up. "You could have lived a long life, snorting all the coke you wanted off strippers' asses, but no. You had to fuck it all up. And, now you will die because of your decision."

I walked over to the workbench. Slowly, I scanned the hand tools that were laid out on the table. Manny needed to be made an example of. He wasn't worthy of a swift death. Fuckers like him deserved slow suffering.

"Take the rag out. I want to hear his excuse." I glanced over my shoulder. Eddie pulled the rag free of Manny's mouth.

"I– I– It's not like that, Boss," Manny stammered. "I swear."

"You fucking swear?" I shouted, grabbing the first tool my hand touched– the hammer. With all my might, I threw the hammer at Manny, striking him in the chest. He yelled in pain. "That is just an inkling of what you're going to feel when I am done with you."

"Boss, I didn't mean to," Manny sobbed. His whininess only added to my anger.

"Who'd you order the women through?" I asked, turning my back to him to look over the tools once more.

"He'll kill me if he finds out I told you."

"He'll kill you?" I chuckled. "You're dead anyway. If you tell me who, I might make your death swifter."

Not happening, I thought picking up the shaving knife.

"Tino. Tino Romano," he blurted.

"Tino Romano," I repeated.

Tino Romano was a name I was familiar with. His name popped up on my radar several times. He had connections on the east coast, keeping me from touching him. A brother who was a caporegime for the De Santos Family. Tino had used his brother's name to get things out of life: money, drugs, cars, even shares in casinos.

It wasn't that I was afraid of Tino Romano. It was that I respected the De Santos Family. Doing anything to Tino could cause a domino effect. One I preferred to avoid; however, if Tino thought for a second I would standby and allow sex trafficking, he had another thing coming. Vegas was my city. And no one fucked with my city.

"Looks like it is time to pay Tino a visit," I looked at Eddie. "Tell Niccolai and the others, business meeting in thirty minutes. And no one better be late!"

"You got it, Boss," he said, walking across the garage. He looked at me. "Want me to–"

"Send in Vincent. It's time he earned his keep." Eddie grinned at my words, opened the door, and left. "Now where were we Manny?"

"Hoping you'd let me go, Boss," Manny whispered.

"Not a chance in hell," I groaned. "How many women did you dispose of?"

"A few– Just a few."

"How many!" My voice boomed throughout the garage.

"Fifty."

His confession made my stomach knot. Fifty women had lost their lives. If only I hadn't gone to the wedding. I could have prevented it.

"You killed fifty women in two days?" I gritted through clenched teeth. "Fifty fucking women!"

"It wasn't supposed to be. Was just supposed to be a woman or two, but for one-hundred K, I got a truck full, which was fifty."

"You're un-fucking-believable. A real piece of shit. You know that right?" I turned and faced him. He lowered his eyes to the floor.

"I've been a sick fuck for a long time," he admitted softly.

"You're going to give me information on Tino and then I'm sending you to meet the man upstairs. Understood?"

"I can– I can change. I swear."

"There's no changing a sick fuck like you," Flint muttered. Manny glanced over at Flint. He looked like he wanted to say something to Flint, but kept his mouth shut.

"You want to know how to hit Tino hard?" Manny asked, turning his attention back to me. I nodded my head. "He has a niece arriving from Jersey. You can use her to get to him. If she comes up missing, he will–"

"Why the fuck would I want to kidnap a woman? Did Eddie hit you so hard that you forgot why the fuck you're here? I don't fucking hurt women!"

"Not hurt her," he shook his head. "Just take her. His brother will take care of the rest if you make it look like Tino hurt her."

"I'm not taking advice from a sick fuck prick like you."

"Or use her to get Tino to do anything you command of him."

"Shut the–" Flint growled, but I held my hand up.

Manny's words piqued my interest. Tino had his paws on a few casinos I wanted. So using the niece as leverage could work to my advantage. However, at the end of the day, what I really wanted was the fucker dead. But how the hell was I going to kidnap the niece without bringing heat to my front door from the brother in New Jersey, who worked for De Santos?

Ah. I could tip off the sharks– De Santos and the brother– for Tino's role in the fifty women being murdered.

"Command him, eh?" I smirked, deciding to worry about the details of the plan later. "There are a few things I could think of. I could always return her later."

"Could make her work for you, Boss," Flint suggested.

"Make her work for me?" I groaned, looking at him like he lost his fucking mind.

Flint had been with me for a while. He knew my rules and

knew how I felt about prostitution. There was no way in hell I'd kidnap a woman and make her a sex slave.

"Yeah. Why not? I mean, be kinda nice to work with a chick for once, Boss," Flint shrugged. "She could handle the issues we have with women since we can't hurt no woman."

"Oh," I chuckled. "So, not a call girl?"

"What? Never," Flint shook his head. "Boss, that's not how we roll."

"So, a kidnapper turned boss type of thing?" I chuckled just as the door opened. Vincent walked in.

"Hey, Boss," Vincent said, closing the door. "You called for me?"

"Yep. Time to earn your keep." I headed over to the door and opened it. "I'll think on your coworker request, Flint."

"Thanks, Boss!" Flint called out cheerfully as I stepped outside, closing the door behind me and sealing Manny's fate.

Time for a sitdown.

CHAPTER SEVEN

SOFIA

The entire flight from Jersey to Vegas, I only had two thoughts. One was of the very sexy Antonio Berlusconi, who had haunted my dreams since the wedding. My second thought was how I was going to Vanish. Literally. There was no way in hell I was staying with Tino. I should have ratted his ass out years ago but I was trying to be a good daughter and spare my father the heartache of knowing exactly who his baby brother was.

Stupid ass, I cursed myself. *But at least Rosaline doesn't have to deal with this.*

The plane had landed fifteen minutes ago, and we were finally deboarding. I walked down the long hallway towards my doom. The other passengers rushed by me, hurrying to catch their next plane or darting off to baggage claim. Either way, I stepped off to the side, allowing everyone and anyone to blaze past me.

"Maybe I should play some slots?" I looked at the slot machines that were a few feet from me. "Could kill some time."

My phone decided to ring right then. I fished my phone out of my pocket. Reading the name on the screen, I groaned as I answered the call.

"Hi, Papa," I replied, walking past the slot machines.

"You landed. Why didn't you call or text me?" His tone was flat. I hadn't even been in Vegas for an hour and already he was upset with me.

"They just let us off the plane."

"You could have turned on your phone once you landed," he informed me.

I could inform him of the F.C.C. rules on cell phones, but it would be pointless. He was used to getting his way. Whatever facts I retorted with, he'd simply deny them then argue more.

"Yes, Papa." I bit back a groan.

"Are you at baggage claim yet?"

Yes, I flew there. I just told you I just left the damn plane.

"Almost," I said, picking up my step.

"Hurry. I don't want you walking around by yourself. I should have had Carlo fly with you."

"Papa, I'm fine. I'm almost to baggage claim."

"Affrettatevi," he growled.

Hurry up, I repeated in English and rolled my eyes.

"Di fretta, Papa."

I am… You impatient ass.

"Go to baggage claim. Tino's men will be waiting for you. Get your luggage after you are with them. Capisci?"

"Capisco."

"Ciao," he said, ending the call before I could respond.

Typical of him lately. There was a time when my father was the man I looked up to. I couldn't wait to get home from school and tell him all about my day. Or go out for ice cream with him and my sisters. Times used to be good. However, the past year he had turned into someone I barely recognized.

I hated being in the same room with him. He was always on edge, paranoid about the slightest things, and flew off the deep end at the drop of a hat. The warm fuzzy feeling towards my father was a thing of the past. I didn't even like calling him *Papa* anymore. I only did it for two reasons. One, out of habit. Two, to keep the peace amongst the family.

"Baggage claim…" an announcement said over the intercom. I didn't catch the rest of the message, but it was enough to snap me free from memory lane.

I followed the signs and the herd of people until eventually, I stood in baggage claim. The place was huge and a madhouse. How the hell was I supposed to find my uncle's goons? It wasn't like they'd be holding up a sign with my–

"I'll be damn," I chuckled, looking at a white poster with *Romano* written on it. The guy holding it wore a nice, black tailored suit. There were two guys next to him. They were also dressed to impress. "Found you."

I walked over to the three men. One looked super familiar. The taller of the three. His eyes widened when he saw me.

"Hello," I said, setting my carry-on bag down.

"Have any other bags?" the familiar-looking guy asked me.

"Two." I held up two fingers. He nodded and looked at the other two guys.

"Go with her and grab her bags. I'm going to call the boss real quick," he gestured at the two guys.

"We're on it," the one who hadn't spoken replied, picking up my carry-on bag. "We'll follow you."

"Alrighty then." Something was off about the three. I wasn't sure what exactly. I just knew deep in my gut something was up.

The two guys followed me over to carousel three, where my luggage would be. I looked back over my shoulder. The familiar guy was a few feet from us.

"We have a problem, Boss," I heard him say. Our eyes met and he stared at me with intensity. "You're never going to believe it if I told you."

"Which one is yours?" one of the other guys asked.

I wanted to focus on the other guy's phone call but pulled my attention away long enough to point out my hot pink suitcases. When I looked back at the other guy, he was nowhere to be found.

"Let's go," one of them said, rolling my suitcase several feet in front of me and the other guy. The other guy didn't budge until I started to walk. Then he walked protectively behind me.

Typical goon, I groaned to myself.

A few minutes later, my things were being loaded into the back of a black SUV. Another guy in a suit stood by the opened back passenger door. He stared at me so intensely I thought he was going to burn a hole into me.

"Let's go," the familiar guy said, gesturing at the open door.

"Can I ride up front?" I asked. He shook his head.

"No. Sit in the back," he replied.

"The front." I crossed my arms in front of my chest.

"The back. End of discussion."

"What's wrong with sitting up front?"

"Sit in the back…" he groaned. "Please."

The other three guys chuckled, earning them a glare. They quickly silenced.

"It's easier to not argue with him. Get in," the guy standing next to the passenger door replied. Then gestured with his head for me to climb in. "He won't ask nicely again."

The last of his words came out harsh. They were a threat. I found myself swallowing an invisible lodge in my throat and climbing in the backseat.

"At least she isn't a dumb bitch," one of them stated.

"Watch your words about her. Boss will kill you if you call her outside her name," the familiar guy growled. "Understood?"

"Understood," they all responded, getting into the vehicle.

The familiar guy sat up front in the passenger seat. The guy who held the sign got in the driver's seat. The other two goons sat on both sides of me. With their large bodies, the car felt like a sardine can.

I kept my mouth shut as our journey to my uncle's house began. They small-talked amongst themselves. Mostly about sports but then their conversation piqued my interest.

"Miami was such a shit show," the familiar guy muttered.

"That's what happens at weddings. They're all shit shows," the guy to my right laughed.

Miami? Wedding?

"You've been bitching about that trip for the past three days," the guy to my left shook his head and chuckled. "So the place got shot up a bit. At least you had some excitement. Hell. We were stuck back here dealing with–"

The guy glanced at me then looked forward again.

"We were all business back here," he finished his sentence.

"So your *boss* went to Miami at a wedding recently?" I asked, sitting up in my seat. The guy in the passenger seat tensed. He looked back at me.

My uncle rarely left Vegas. When he did, it was to go to Jersey or Italy. Places with family connections. Miami didn't have any family connections. Not even a second cousin. There was no way in hell my uncle would go to Miami for a wedding. And quite the coincidence that this wedding also got shot up.

The boss they were talking about wasn't my uncle. But who the hell was their boss and what did he want with me?

"How was your flight?" the familiar guy asked, ignoring my question.

"Cut the shit. Where are my uncle's men?" My eyes narrowed in on him. He smirked slightly then chuckled.

"Just sit back and enjoy the ride." He faced forward.

"Don't think so," I shook my head. "Sorry, fellas." I grinned at the two guys sitting beside me. They both looked at me confused.

At the top of my lungs, I screamed. The driver swerved off the road, nearly crashing into a semi-truck. He quickly gained control of the car. The familiar guy turned in his chair. His eyes were like lasers on me. Meanwhile, the two in the back with me grimaced and covered their ears.

"Stop screaming or we'll shut you up!" the familiar guy shouted over my screaming.

I shook my head and screamed more.

"Shut her up!" the guy yelled.

"How? We can't hurt her!" the guy to my right shouted.

"Cover her mouth!" the familiar guy ordered.

The two in the back grabbed me. I kicked and screamed more. My legs flailed between the two front seats. Both the driver and the passenger dodged my incoming kicks. The car swerved off the road and the driver slammed the brakes.

My body flew forward towards the dash. A large hand clapped over my mouth while two hands grabbed my arms. The familiar guy wrapped an arm firmly around my ankles.

"We were trying to be nice," he frowned.

"You're kidnapping me!" I screamed against the hand pressed against my mouth.

"Monty, get going. Don't stop again," he growled at the driver, who nodded then pulled back onto the road.

For the rest of the drive, they kept me bound with their hands and arms. No one spoke. Not even the radio was on. The only sounds were that of the city: car horns, emergency vehicle's sirens, and screeching brakes.

"Thank, fuck," the guy to my left muttered when we pulled into a driveway. There was a large black iron gate blocking the driveway. It slowly opened as we approached it.

"Where are we going to put her?" the guy to my right asked.

I uttered curse words against the firm hand covering my mouth, but the bastards heard none of it.

"Since she isn't a *willing* participant anymore, we'll put her in the basement," the guy on the passenger side replied.

Basement? Oh. Hell no, I thought as images of a dark, dingy, smelly basement flashed through my mind. Basements in scary movies were where people got offed. The kind that would wreak death.

I kicked and flailed in protest. The guys held me tighter, keeping me in place.

"Step on it!" the passenger growled.

"Boss will kill me if I speed," the driver– Monty– replied, shaking his head. "He doesn't like any attention brought to the house."

"Should we have blindfolded her?" the guy to the right asked. The vehicle filled with groans.

"Fuck," the passenger muttered. "Let me do the talking when we see the boss."

"I don't want to be the one responsible for that, anyway," Monty shook his head. "Boss is going to lose his shit."

"She'll soften his mood...," the passenger pointed at me with his free hand. "Trust me."

CHAPTER EIGHT

ANTONIO

Eddie had just dropped the bomb of a lifetime on me. His words echoed through my mind as I headed out of my office. I had put off going down to the basement for over an hour. Maybe the reason was shock or maybe it was nerves. Either way, it was time to face the music.

I knocked on the door leading down to the basement.

"Fuck off!" a familiar woman's voice shouted, making me laugh.

"She's a ray of sunshine," Niccolai chuckled. I glanced back at him and grinned.

"Something tells me, we aren't welcomed." I turned the doorknob and slowly opened it.

"Want me to go first, Boss?" Niccolai asked. I shook my head and walked down the steps.

"I'll kill you if you lay one fucking finger on me! I swear to God!" Sofia shrieked.

When I made it to the bottom of the steps, My eyes landed on her. A deep growl escaped me. She was in the far corner, tied up to a chair, facing the wall with her back to me.

"Why the fuck is she in *time-out*?" I asked, storming over to her.

"She was beating the shit out of us, Boss," Eddie replied behind me. Monty and Howard, who were standing guard next to

Sofia, nodded in agreement. Monty's eye looked slightly swollen. Howard's face had several scratch marks across it.

"I barely touched you, you fucking cry babies!" Sofia screamed.

"Are you hurt?" I grabbed her chair and turned it to where she was now facing me. Her eyes widened and her cheeks reddened as she looked up at me.

"Wh– What?" she stammered.

"Did they hurt you?" She shook her head in response. "Good," I smiled then looked at Monty. "Untie her."

"Are you sure, Boss? She might try to–" Monty replied but closed his mouth when I glared.

"You got it, Boss." He quickly untied the ropes from her wrists. She brought her hands in front of her and rubbed her wrists.

"Were they too tight?" I asked, dropping to a knee and grabbing one of her hands. She tensed at my touch. "Does that hurt?"

Our eyes met and she blushed again.

"No. I'm fine. Really," she whispered.

"Good."

"There you go," Monty said, freeing her legs from the chair.

"Thanks," she said sarcastically as she glared up at him.

"Just doing my job." He held his hands up in surrender and stood tall. "No hard feelings?"

"You fucking kidnapped me! So, yes, hard feelings," she frowned. Wasn't my best decision, but I laughed. Now her eyes were narrowed in on me.

"Sorry, Beautiful. You can blame me for both," I brought her hand up to my lips and kissed it softly; hoping to buy me some forgiveness from her.

"Why are you here?" she asked, narrowing her eyes on me. Forgiveness seemed like something I was going to have to work for.

I stood up and offered my hand to her. She stared at it for some time before shaking her head.

"First…explain," she sassed.

"Very well." I looked around for another chair. "Someone grab me a chair."

"I'm on it, Boss," Howard replied, running across the room and up the stairs.

"Want something to eat or drink?" I offered.

"Nope," she shook her head. "Just want to know why you are here."

"Well…"

I'm a mob boss and your uncle is a piece of shit! That would be the correct answer; however, I had a feeling that wouldn't be what she wanted to hear. She was probably traumatized by the guys snatching her up… even though it didn't sound too eventful until they got her into the car.

"Well, what?" Sofia prompted.

"Got one, Boss!" Monty called out as he came barrel-assing down the steps and over to us. He set the chair down then took a few steps back.

"You guys can go upstairs," I gestured towards the steps.

"You sure you want us to leave, Boss?" Niccolai asked.

"Yeah. I think I'm safe," I chuckled, earning me another death stare from Sofia.

"Just because you're hot doesn't mean I won't fuck you up," she pointed a finger at me. The guys chuckled around me while I grinned. There was something extremely sexy about her threatening me.

"Promise?" I smirked. Her eyes widened and her cheeks turned bright red. "Yeah, I'll be good. You guys go upstairs. I'll yell if she gets too rough."

The guys chuckled again at her expense. Her face was now the color of a tomato. She looked absolutely mortified.

"Sorry, Love. I'll behave," I offered her an apologetic smile. "Leave us."

The guys acknowledged my order then headed upstairs, leaving me alone with the beautiful Sofia.

"Where were we?" I asked, sitting down in the chair. Sofia's eyes lowered down to where our knees touched. She slowly brought her gaze back up to me.

"Were you responsible for the wedding fiasco?" she asked softly.

"No."

"Did you plan on kidnapping me at the wedding?"

"What?" I laughed and shook my head. "No. Didn't know you were who you were until a few minutes ago."

"And who am I?"

Her question surprisingly made my heart skip a few beats. It wasn't like me to be nervous to speak my mind. However, there was just something about Sofia. She had been on my mind constantly since Miami. I even debated on digging up information on her then flying to wherever she lived and *coincidentally* running into her.

We hadn't known each other for long, but the short amount of time I had known her had made me want to be a better man. She made me uneasy about being who I was and the life I lived.

"Earth to you," Sofia waved her hand in front of my face.

"Tino Romano's niece," I replied cooley.

"I see." Her eyebrow raised. "So you meant to kidnap me to do what exactly?"

"To come to an understanding with your uncle."

"What'd the dick do now?" she muttered, rolling her eyes and uncrossing her arms.

"Nothing that can't be fixed by a little family persuasion."

"And that'd be me?" I nodded in response. "What do you plan on doing to me?"

Her soft words coming from her plush lips made my dick jerk hard. Fuck. She was so fucking sexy.

I adjusted in my seat.

"Ignoring me on purpose?" she mused.

"Trying to behave, if you must know." When her cheeks reddened again, I chuckled. "You asked."

"Behave?" she sucked in a sharp breath.

I nodded and looked down at my hard-on that was pressing against the inside of my slacks. Sofia's eyes lowered down to my pants. Her eyes widened and she bit her bottom lip before looking back up at me.

"See my problem?" I smirked.

"Looks like a very *big* problem," she whispered. Her tongue ran across her bottom lip. My dick throbbed at her seductive gesture.

"A problem that seems to happen only when you're around," I admitted.

"Is it wrong of me to want to help you with that problem..." Her eyes met my gaze. "even though you kidnapped me?"

"What if I apologized sincerely? Would that make helping

me with my problem easier for you?"

"Fuck," she moaned. Her chest raised and lowered as her breaths quickened. The desire in her eyes made me want to pin her against the nearest wall and fuck her senseless.

"If you keep looking at me like that, I'm going to forget my manners, Sofia."

"Mmm," she moaned. "Promise?"

"Fuck," I groaned, gripping my knees to keep myself grounded. I was on the brink of forgetting all logic. Tino's niece or not, I needed Sofia Romano like I needed air.

"Going to make me make the first move?" she asked, standing up then straddling my waist. Her arms wrapped around my neck and she ground down against my dick.

"Fuck, Baby," I moaned squeezing her ass with both of my hands. "You're so fucking sexy."

"Antonio, I need you," she whispered warmly against my ear.

"You can have me."

"Fuck me."

CHAPTER NINE

SOFIA

Insanity. Fucking insanity would be my plea if what happened next ever left this room. It was like my body was possessed. I should be in fear for my life. The man had me kidnapped by his goons. Yet, fear was the last thing on my mind. I craved Antonio like something fierce. The way I felt towards him at the wedding was nothing compared to now.

When my chair had turned and I came face-to-face with him, my entire world seemed to stop. The universe had crossed our paths again. It was as though fate was hinting at me that Antonio was *the one*.

And now as I straddled his lap so many intense raw emotions flooded through me. And not a single emotion told me to run from him. They all screamed for me to give myself to him completely.

"Sofia," Antonio moaned, grabbing my hips. "I thought you wanted answers?"

"Later," I whimpered. The need for him was growing too strong. "I need you now."

"But what about–"

I didn't let him finish his sentence. Talking was the last thing I wanted to do. My lips crashed against his. My tongue greedily pressed past his lips and into his mouth. I worried he might push me away, but I needed him.

His arm wrapped around my waist, his tongue stroked mine

tenderly. The taste of coffee and caramel exploded in my mouth. I moaned into his mouth as my body melted against his.

My hips circled slowly matching the pace of our kiss. Antonio's hands pushed my hips downward, pressing his hard-on against the very spot I needed him. My pussy throbbed and ached to be filled.

"Please," I whimpered absently.

"So fucking sexy," Antonio growled. He nipped at my bottom lip and tugged gently. I sucked in a sharp breath as desire and warmth filled my core.

"Antonio, please," I begged.

"Are you sur–"

I bit his bottom lip hard. He slapped my ass. I winced from the pain and throbbed from pleasure all in one breath. It was the most erotic feeling I had ever experienced.

"Either…" I pulled away just enough to look him in the eye, "Either fuck me now or find someone who will."

The look in his eyes shifted from lust-filled to predator ready to devour their prey.

"I'm going to fuck that pretty little pussy until you vow that it's mine."

He might as well have opened a cage to a pack of wild wolves. I came unglued by his words. I grabbed the hem of my shirt, pulled it up and over my head, then removed my bra. My breasts bounced inches from his lips teasingly.

"Fuck," he moaned as he watched me stand up and make waste of my shoes, socks, and pants. Now, I stood in front of him with only a black lacy thong.

"Ball is in your court, Mr. Berlusconi," I said vixen-like.

Antonio stood and quickly undressed. My mouth gaped

open with each inch of skin he bared. The man was the definition of perfection. I wanted to lick every inch of his body… twice.

When he slid his pants down and his cock sprung free, I swallowed hard. Antonio was huge.

"Fuck," I breathed, staring down at his hard-on.

Antonio grabbed the base of his shaft. My mouth watered as I watched anxiously, hoping for a taste.

"Like what you see, Baby?" he asked, stroking his cock. I nodded. "Tell me what you want me to do?"

I wanted him deep down my throat, but I also wanted him buried inside my pussy. The wild urge to feel his cock between my thighs outweighed my need to suck him off. If I was lucky, we'd get a round two and I could see just how much of him I could take in my mouth.

"Fuck me, Mr. Berlusconi," I grinned, turning around. Antonio's arm wrapped around my waist, he spun me to face him. He shook his head and smirked.

"I want to see that beautiful face while I fuck you."

"Mmm. Yes, sir."

Antonio lifted me up by my ass. My legs wrapped around his waist. He reached between us and positioned the tip of his cock at my entrance.

"You're so wet, Baby," Antonio moaned.

My heart skipped a beat and I sucked in an anxious breath, patiently waiting.

"Antonio," I said, rocking my hips.

"Mmm. That's it, Baby. Show me how bad you want me."

"Fuck!" I screamed, when he thrust forward, burying his cock deep inside me without warning.

My pussy stretched to fit his size. Pain and pleasure ricocheted throughout my body. Wave after wave of emotion struck me.

Antonio held still. His eyes locked on mine. Worry sketched on his face.

"Are you– Were you a–" he stammered, making me giggle.

"No. You're just fucking huge." He replied to my words with a cocky grin. "If you're so into yourself then you don't need me."

"What?" he looked at me in disbelief.

"It's a joke, Lover Boy," I smiled and nipped gently at his bottom lip. His cock throbbed inside me. Antonio and I both moaned from the movement.

"You're so tight, Baby."

"Stretch me."

"Fuck," he groaned.

He carried me a few short feet over to the wall. My back was now pressed against the wall. I looked up at him to find him grinning down at me. Not a typical grin. This was a grin that made a shiver run down my spine and my pussy wet.

"Remember what I said." He kissed up the side of my neck.

Antonio's soft kisses made me close my eyes to bask in the intimacy. Such a simple gesture, yet, it would have brought me to my knees had I been standing.

"Remember what?" I whispered.

He kissed my lips gently and pulled away. I opened my eyes to see what had pulled his attention away. He was staring at me. Intensity filled his gaze.

"By the time I'm done with this tight pussy, you're going to vow to be mine," he said huskily. There was no hint of amusement or cockiness. He meant the words he spoke.

"Yours?" I asked sheepishly. My cheeks burned. Not from

embarrassment but from the unknown possibility of... romance?

"Tell me you didn't feel the attraction at the wedding?" He began to pull his cock out of me. I started to whimper and protest, but he slid deep inside me once more.

My arms tightened around his neck, and I sucked in a sharp breath. He stroked his cock in and out of my pussy. Each time my pussy stretched around him. The pain became an unbearable pleasure. Etched in my mind for eternity.

"Did you not feel it?" he asked, freezing in place.

"Antonio," I whimpered.

"Tell me and I'll keep fucking you," he replied. "Even if you didn't feel it."

"No–" I shook my head. A look of disappointment crossed over his face. "Stop pouting and let me finish my sentence," I giggled.

"Go on," he chuckled.

"I definitely felt it. If things hadn't gone down the way they had, I was going to get your number."

"Is that so?"

"Mmhmm."

"I have a confession."

"What's that?"

"I had every intention of releasing Tino's niece, but since it's you..." He took a deep breath. "I'm never going to let you go, Sofia."

CHAPTER TEN

ANTONIO

Why the fuck did I pick right now to confess this to her? I groaned to myself. I should have just stuck to fucking her then figured out everything else later. Balls deep inside her wasn't the time to have this conversation.

"You sure it's not the pussy getting to you?" she giggled quietly. I rolled my eyes and laughed.

"You think that's why I want you?" I smirked.

"I mean, men have done some crazy stuff for pussy."

I pulled my dick out leaving only the tip inside her. She tensed and looked up at me with pleading eyes.

"Antonio," she said softly. "Please."

"I'm not going anywhere, Beautiful," I assured her. "We can have that other conversation later."

"What about the vow?" she smiled innocently.

This woman was going to be the death of me. The way she had me wrapped around her finger without even trying. Or how she had made me hers without declaring it. None of it made sense; however, it all felt right.

I'm a fucking pussy, I scolded myself. Maybe after we fucked things would make sense. Or maybe I'd be an even bigger goner.

"Stop," Sofia sighed.

"What?"

Fuck. Had I said all that shit out loud?

"You look deep in thought and scared shitless," she laughed. "Fuck me senseless and we can worry about everything else later."

"Fuck," I moaned.

"Unless you want someone else to fuck me," she teased sultry-like.

"Never," I growled, slamming balls deep inside her without hesitation. Her screams echoed throughout the room.

"Anton–" She didn't get a chance to finish her word.

I braced one hand against the wall and slammed in and out of her hard and fast. My balls slapped against her with each thrust. Her tits bounced from the force and Sofia's heavenly moans and screams filled my ears.

Her warm, tight pussy squeezed my cock and stretched as I fucked her. My balls tightened as an orgasm threatened to fill her pussy.

Too soon, I grunted to myself. I wasn't ready for this to end.

"Pinch your nipples," I growled. Sofia's hands raised to her tits. With two fingers she pinched her blush-colored nipples. A moan slipped past her lips and her pussy tightened.

"Antonio," she gasped.

"Pinch them harder," I gritted between clenched teeth.

She pinched her nipples harder. She whimpered in pain and bucked her hips wildly against me. My rhythm quickened and became more sporadic as I pounded in and out of Sofia. My need to fill her with my hot cum became almost insatiable.

"Antonio, I'm– I'm– I'm going to come!" Sofia panted. Her nails dug into my back, giving me the final push.

"Antonio!" she screamed as her orgasm took hold of her.

"Sofia!" I roared, tightening my hold around her. I gave one final forceful thrust before releasing every last drop of my cum deep inside her.

"Fuck," I moaned. My chest rose and lowered rapidly.

"Mmhmm," Sofia giggled softly. She laid her head on my shoulder. "Mmm. I needed that."

"Did you, Baby?" I asked, kissing the side of her neck.

"I did."

"Good." I rubbed her back then lowered her to her feet. She looked up at me with sleep-filled eyes. "Let's get you to bed."

"No. I'm good," she yawned. We both laughed.

"Your body says otherwise, ma'am," I chuckled then lifted her up in my arms. She wrapped her arms around my neck and giggled.

"What are you doing?" She looked up at me innocently.

"Taking you upstairs so you can go to sleep."

"Am I no longer your captive?" she grinned.

Fuck, I groaned to myself.

Kidnapping Tino's niece to get to him hadn't seemed like the best idea at the time. Then finding out Sofia was the niece complicated things and tipped my moral compass. And now I had a taste of what I had been craving since the wedding— her. There was no turning back. I couldn't just let her go but I didn't want to hold her against her will either. Her staying needed to be her decision. Even if the thought of her leaving made me stir-crazy.

I looked down at her and smiled.

"Ball is in your court, Beautiful."

CHAPTER ELEVEN

SOFIA

The sun peeked through the gap in the curtains, waking me from my slumber. I turned my head away from the light and snuggled deeper into the plush comforter. It smelled of Antonio. I couldn't help but take a deep breath, basking in his scent.

Images of the night prior flashed through my mind. So much had happened in a short amount of time. I went from being abducted against my will to freely giving myself to Antonio.

"Mmm," I smiled.

Antonio was everything I wanted in a man. He was sexy, strong, powerful, and incredible in bed. He did things to my mind, body, and soul that I never thought imagined.

The way he made me feel and the way I craved him, both excited and terrified me. It was a dangerous game I was playing. Deep down I knew I needed to leave. This was the last place I needed to be; however, it was also the only place on Earth I desired to be.

Regardless of how I felt it wasn't safe for me to stay. A war would come to Antonio's front door because there was no way in hell my uncle or father would let Antonio get away with kidnapping me. Willingly or not. It was the principle of the matter. I was a Romano. No one went against our family.

"Ugh. Such a tangled fucking web," I groaned, kicking at the covers. It was childish to throw a tantrum but damn it, I wanted my cake and to eat it too.

With a heavy sigh, I sat up and looked around the room. The room was huge and screamed masculine playboy. I rolled my eyes at the thought of Antonio being with another woman. He had the good looks and charms so of course he probably had been with dozens of women.

"Mother fucker," I grumped.

Knock. Knock. Knock.

"What?" I shouted.

"Message from the boss," a man replied from the other side of the door. I

"What's the message?"

"Uh. It's not a verbal message," he said, piquing my interest. I climbed out of bed and made my way over to the door while pulling my hair back up into a ponytail. I flipped on the light and opened the door.

Standing there was a young guy– maybe my age– wearing a black suit and tie. His hair was slicked back. In his hands was a tray of food and a cup of coffee.

"Would this be the message?" I grinned.

The guy's eyes widened as he looked at me. The coffee cup clinked against the plate beneath it as his hands trembled. He closed his eyes and lowered his head.

"Fuck. He's going to kill me." His voice was low and filled with fear.

"What? Why?" My eyes lowered to look and see what had scared him. A chill ran down my spine and a terrifying scream left me.

Naked. I was butt-ass naked.

With the thoughts of Antonio dancing through my head, I hadn't thought to put clothes on before I opened the door. Hell, to be honest, I had forgotten I didn't have any on. Antonio had carried me to his room after our fun and I had drifted peacefully to sleep.

Heavy footsteps sounded down the hallway. They were coming our way and fast. I quickly closed the door, shielding myself from further embarrassment. My back pressed against the door as I stood mortified.

"What the fuck happened?" Antonio's words were loud, deep, and harsh. The type of tone that could command Satan himself.

"She– She was–" the guy stammered. "Boss, I swear on everything, I didn't know she'd answer the door like that."

"Like what?" Antonio growled.

"Naked," the guy replied softly.

"You saw her naked?" Antonio shouted right before something slammed against the bedroom door, scaring the shit out of me. I screamed.

"Sofia!" Antonio shouted.

The door flung open without warning. My body jolted from the sudden force and I fell to the floor.

"Sofia!" Antonio cried out. He stormed into the room. When he saw me, he picked me up and held me in his arms. His eyes were filled with worry.

"Are you okay?" he asked softly.

"Mmhmm," I nodded, rubbing my elbow.

"She okay, Boss?" a man asked. He stood out of sight somewhere in the hallway. After Antonio's outburst, I doubted any of them would step foot in this room– if they wanted to live to see another day.

"She's fine!" he growled. I couldn't help but groan and roll my eyes. "What?" he asked in a softer tone.

"You always so temperamental?" I sighed. Antonio shrugged in response. "It isn't that guy's fault that I opened the door like a fucking idiot."

"What does that mean?" he frowned.

"I was in la-la land when he showed up with the food. Opened the door without even remembering that I was na–" I groaned loudly and tried to climb out of Antonio's hold.

I was still naked. Antonio had seen my body last night but that was different. We were both caught in the moment and only thinking of one thing. Sex. Now, he'd be able to see every flaw.

"Sofia, what's wrong?"

"I'm naked!" I shrieked, swatting at him lightly.

"So?" he chuckled.

"So, I don't want you seeing my…" My words trailed off. Insecurities flooded my mind and I suddenly wished I was anywhere but here.

"Sofia," he said tenderly. "You're beautiful."

"No. I'm not," I shook my head. He sighed then carried me over to the bed. He laid me down gently. "Be right back."

He walked across the room and stepped into the hallway. I couldn't hear what was being said. I just hoped he wouldn't reprimand the guy like my father would.

"Don't hurt him!" I screamed in the direction of the door. Antonio poked his head in the door and chuckled.

"I won't hurt him," he smiled.

"Promise?"

"Yes. I promise, Beautiful."

"No one else either," I added. I had a sneaky suspicion he'd find a way to get around the promise. I held out my pinky. Antonio's eyebrow rose. "Pinky-promise me that you and no one else will hurt him."

"Pinky-promise?"

"Mmhmm. It's not his fault I was a fucking dumbass and forgot I didn't have clothes on." He frowned at my words. "What? I was."

"I don't want you talking bad about yourself again." His words were a cross between romantic and a command.

I sucked in a sharp breath and bit my bottom lip. My thighs squeezed together as my pussy throbbed, begging to be taken by Antonio.

Fuck, I'm hopeless.

"Understood?" he asked.

I fought the urge to spread my legs and beg him to take me. There were more important things to deal with right now. Things like the poor bastard in the hallway who was about to be offed because of my stupidity.

"I won't say anything bad if you promise to not let anything happen to him," I bargained.

Antonio stared at me long and hard. Finally, he nodded and laughed.

"Deal. But don't go back on your word," he pointed at me.

"I'm a lady of my word, Sir," I informed him sassily.

"I trust you." He stuck his head out into the hallway. "Troy, thank Sofia. She just saved your life."

"Thank you, Sofia," the guy said from the hallway. Antonio grinned smugly.

"The next person to see what's mi–" Antonio frowned at his own words. "The next person to see Sofia's body is a dead man.

Understood?"

"Yes, Boss," the men in the hallway said in unison.

"Give me that," Antonio ordered. The tray was handed to him then the door closed. "Wasn't sure what'd you ate so I had the chef make you a bit of everything," he said walking over to the bed.

"I appreciate that," I whispered. "Um… may I…"

"May you what?" he asked with his eyebrow raised.

"Um… I was woken up by the door. Can I freshen up before I eat?" I asked, slightly mortified. Guess it was better than saying *I have to pee.*

"Oh." His eyes widened. "By all means," he gestured at a door.

I quickly hopped off the bed and scurried off to the bathroom. A few minutes later, I walked back into the room feeling a thousand times better. Antonio was sitting in the recliner in the corner of the room. The tray of food was at the foot of the bed.

"Hey," I said, causing myself to groan internally. I sounded like a fucking idiot.

"Hey," he chuckled, then stood. "Hungry?"

"Mmhmm," I nodded, climbing onto the bed carefully.

Antonio walked over to the bed and picked up the tray. Once I was settled with my back against the headboard, he placed the tray on my lap. He took the lid off the food. Everything looked and smelled like heaven.

"Are you going to eat?" I asked, looking up at him.

"I usually only drink a cup of coffee."

"Oh."

"But if you don't want to eat alone, I'll have them bring something up for me to eat."

"No," I shook my head. "I don't want to interrupt your routine."

"I assure you, you aren't interrupting anything, Sofia," he smiled. "Want me to eat with you?"

"No. It's okay," I replied, picking up a piece of bacon and taking a small bite out of it. The taste was just how it looked and smelled. "Mmm. This tastes so good." I took another bite.

"When's the last time you ate?" Antonio chuckled. I shrugged at his words.

"Yesterday around breakfast time. I didn't get a chance to eat lunch because I was packing my stuff to come to this God-forsaken city. For dinner, I was on a plane and not in the mood to eat, and then I was picked up by your goons and brought here where.... Well, food was the last thing on my mind," I admitted.

"Yeah, sorry about that. I should have been a better host."

"Oh, you were," I smirked, making him chuckle.

"You weren't fed; therefore, I was a pretty shitty host, Sofia."

"You fed me in other ways."

"Naughty ass," he grinned.

"Going to sit next to me or just keep standing over me?" I asked, patting the spot beside me.

Antonio laughed then took off his jacket and draped it over the recliner. I ate another piece of bacon while he made his way around the bed. He climbed into bed and sat next to me, facing me.

"Food tastes okay?" he asked, glancing at the tray.

"Bacon is delish," I replied, taking another bite.

"What about the other stuff?" he looked down at the food.

"How'd you know I loved strawberries?" I grabbed the fork and stabbed a strawberry. I took a bite of the strawberry and melted. It wasn't too sweet or too sour.

"I didn't. They're my favorite fruit so I tend to assume everyone loves them," he admitted with a chuckle.

"Ah. I see." I took another bite. "So, what's the game plan with me?"

His body tensed. The entire vibe of the room shifted from pleasant to all business. Or at least that was the feeling it was giving me.

"Your uncle has been informed of your location," he replied coolie.

"He'll come for you," I sighed, looking up at him.

"He won't," he assured me.

"How can you be so sure?"

"Because right now your uncle is jumping through hoops to ensure that your father doesn't catch wind that you've been..." His words trailed off.

"Kidnapped," I said, finishing his statement. He nodded.

"Yes. Kidnapped."

"And, why wouldn't my uncle just tell my father where I am so I can be rescued?"

"Because your uncle fucked up and now fears someone more than your father and his connections."

My eyes searched Antonio's for signs that I should fear him. Was he really a greater threat than my father and his associates? Nothing about Antonio made me want to run away. Even now, as his hostage, I didn't have the urge to escape. In fact, it was the total opposite. For the first time in my life, I felt truly comfortable and safe.

"I find that hard to believe," I admitted, picking up the glass of orange juice. "If you're a greater threat than my father then that would mean I'm in danger."

I took a long, slow sip of my orange juice. Antonio watched me like a hawk the entire time. I lowered my glass down to the tray.

"Am I in danger being around you?" I asked flatly.

"No," he replied without hesitation.

"Thought so."

"But that doesn't mean the rest of the world isn't when I'm around."

His words would have scared most women. They would have trembled in fear; however, his words did the opposite for me. They ignited a fire deep in my core. A fire created from lust and raw desire. A fire that burned stronger with every second shared between Antonio and me.

Logically, I knew I should run. He was warning me of the type of man he was. However, to me, he was a man whose bad-boy charm, powerful aura, and wicked good looks had me wrapped around his finger without trying. He wasn't dangerous because he could kill me. He was dangerous because he could destroy the one thing I never gave to anyone. My heart.

"Do you plan on letting me go?" I wondered, cocking my head slightly to the side.

"No," he stated. "I told myself I was going to let you go, but I can't."

"Because of my uncle?"

He laughed and shook his head.

"No, because I'm a selfish asshole and want you all to my-self." His words caused me to suck in a sharp breath. My grip on the fork tightened and the room suddenly seemed too small. "However, if you told me to let you go, I would do it in a heartbeat."

"But?" I had a feeling there would be more to just simply letting me go.

"Smart lady," he chuckled. "I'd want to know where you were. If you were okay. Who you were with. So on and so forth."

"Which would mean?" I prompted softly.

"I'd keep tabs on you and fight to make you mine."

"I see," I managed to say, fighting back the nerves that were rising up in me.

"Scared?" I looked at him and frowned.

"Are you serious?" I laughed. "Why would that scare me?"

"Maybe because I'm a complete stranger, who hasn't been able to stop thinking about you since the wedding. And now you're a… guest at my house."

"Guest?" I giggled. "Hostage. When you kidnap someone they become your hostage. Not your guest."

The corner of his lips curled up into a bad-boy smirk. The kind of look that makes panties drop. If I had any on, mine definitely would have hit the floor.

"You're right," he nodded. "But I'm hoping you'd like to change your status from hostage to guest."

"What would become of the situation with my uncle?"

"Well," he took a deep breath. His hand ran through his short hair. "That's a bit complicated."

"Do you plan on killing him?"

"You sure are curious."

"I'm a Romano. Being curious and asking questions is what has kept me alive this long."

CHAPTER TWELVE

ANTONIO

The thought of Sofia having to be on guard her entire life pissed me off. I didn't like her having to worry about someone hurting her. The fact I had her kidnapped only added to my anger. I was no better than the others out there who she was constantly looking out for.

"If you stay here, you won't have to worry about anyone hurting you. Ever," I declared. She looked at me long and hard. Probably searching for the bullshit flag. "I'm serious, Sofia. If you stay with me, you'll never have to worry about anyone hurting you. I swear to that."

"How can you be so sure that no one will hurt me while I'm under your protection?" she asked, plopping a grape into her mouth.

"Because I'll give my last breath before that happens."

Her body tensed and she took a deep breath. I expected her to tell me I was full of shit. However, she didn't. She nodded her head to whatever thought she had then turned her attention to the food.

"Do you like pancakes?" she asked, catching me off guard.

"What?"

"Pancakes." With her fork, she gestured at the stack of pancakes.

"They're alright. Not my favorite," I shrugged.

"Mine either," she said, cutting into them using her fork. "What about waffles?"

"Not really a fan of those either," I admitted as I watched her take a bite of the pancakes. "Thought you didn't like pancakes?"

"I don't but your chef went through the trouble to make them so I'll eat it," she smiled sweetly.

Never had I met a woman like Sofia. Everything about her was mesmerizing. She came from wealth yet she was modest and humble. Most women with the same background as her were materialistic and stuck-up. Not Sofia.

"He won't mind if you toss them," I said. She frowned at my words then took another bite of pancakes. She shook her head and swallowed the bite.

"That's rude." She pointed at me with the fork. "You need to appreciate your people more. Don't end up like my– Just take better care of your people."

I wanted to push her to finish her sentence but I knew if she wanted me to know, she would have told me. So whatever it was, she wasn't ready for me to hear just yet.

"I do take care of my guys. I make sure they get vacations and everything," I stated.

"Vacations?" Her eyes widened. I nodded in response. "Vacations without you?"

"Yes. Vacations without me," I laughed.

"Wow. That's impressive."

"Oh, yeah. Why's that?"

"I just know that most boss– You're a boss, right? I mean, I did some research into you before my life went to hell in a handbasket back in Jersey."

She had looked me up? The thought of her wanting to know

more about me meant I hadn't been wrong about the attraction I felt between us. I was both flattered and turned on.

"And what'd the internet say?" I grinned. She rolled her eyes and laughed.

"Looking you up on the internet would be a sure way to lead the F.B.I. to your doorstep." She took a drink of orange juice then set the glass back down. "I didn't use a computer to ask about you."

"Who'd you ask then?"

Her cheeks reddened and she lowered her eyes to the tray.

"I asked a few close friends of mine if they had heard anything about you," she said, finally looking at me. "Then they asked a few of their close friends. People they could trust."

"I see," I nodded. "And what'd they find out?"

"Just that you're the head of the Berlusconi Family. And like every other boss, not someone to be taken lightly."

"And that didn't scare you?"

"No." There wasn't any hesitation in her answer. The single word was firm and spoke volumes. "Guess I like to play with fire," she shrugged.

"I assure you, Sofia. I won't hurt you."

"You keep saying that." She set her fork down. "But what exactly is your plan with me?"

"I honestly haven't thought one through yet. Wanted your opinion."

"And I get a say in your plan?" She seemed shocked. Not that I could blame her. Mob bosses generally didn't ask the *hostage* for their opinions. It was usually pretty cut and dry.

"Yes. Absolutely."

"You aren't very good at this hostage thing," she giggled, making me laugh.

"I'm starting to realize this."

***

While Sofia ate, we had small-talked about the food and how she slept. Nothing else was mentioned about my plans for her or why I had even kidnapped her. She would teeter on the line but back away from the topic. I didn't push the conversation because I honestly didn't have the answers. I was still trying to figure it all out myself.

"Boss, you okay?" Niccolai asked.

"I'm fine," I said, bringing my attention back to the room.

I was currently sitting at the head of the table in my office. Niccolai sat to my right. Eddie to my left. The rest of the table was filled with two of my other caporegimes– Carlo and Vincent– and soldiers.

Knock. Knock. Knock.

"Come in," I announced. The door opened and Monty stepped inside.

"He's here, Boss," he said.

"Bring him in."

"He doesn't want to enter without his protection party." The room filled with laughter. A smug grin tugged at my lips.

"He can bring a fucking army in here. It won't fucking matter," I spat. The guys cheered. "Tell him to get the fuck in here."

"You got it, Boss," Manny replied then stepped out into the hallway. A few minutes later, heavy footsteps sounded.

"Antonio," Tino acknowledged, walking into my office with his pathetic entourage behind him. A total of six guys. They filed into the room at the far end of the twelve-seat table, where the empty seats were.

Tino wore a shitty pinstripe suit with the pant legs too long.

He looked like he crawled off a seventies porn and was about to go represent someone as their public attorney. The slob had no decency or self-respect.

I didn't respond to him. I simply gestured at the empty seats. He sat down then four of his goons sat down with two remaining behind him standing.

"Where's my niece?" he asked, looking around the room.

"She's safe," I replied with my eyes narrowed in on him. I still couldn't believe that beautiful Sofia was related to this ugly piece of shit.

"How do I know I can trust you?"

"You don't," I smirked. He muttered something under his breath, but we were too far apart for me to hear.

"I want to see her."

"After we discuss some things." My eyes landed on Monty. I nodded my head and he closed the door.

"You kidnap *my* niece but want me to do things on your terms?" Tino chuckled sarcastically. His goons rolled their eyes and shook their heads.

"You got my memo about Manny, right? Or did you need another memo?" I snarled.

"Yeah. I got it," Tino replied, sitting back in his chair. His entire aura shifted. He went from cocky-shithead to scared shitless.

"Are you sure? We have some other pieces of Manny laying around if my point wasn't understood?"

"No. His face being delivered to my front door got my attention."

"Good," I nodded. "So, here's how this is going to happen. You're going to sign over all rights to any and all casinos you have your filthy paws on."

"What?" he scoffed. "Not a fucking chance. I'll just let my brother handle you," he began to stand.

"I'll bet a truck driver's statement that you sit your fat ass back down," I smirked when his eyes landed on me. They were the size of saucers. All color in his face drained. My words had hit their mark.

Slowly, Tino sat back down.

"Which casinos?" he asked, letting out a heavy sigh.

"All of them."

"All of them?" he gritted through clenched teeth.

"*All* of them."

"And I get?" His words made me laugh.

"This isn't really a negotiation. More like an ultimatum."

He stared at me long and hard. His mouth opened as though he wanted to speak, but it closed just as fast. All eyes were on him.

"And if I don't?" he finally asked.

"No hard feelings. I call your brother and let him know about the fifty women you had brought into the city so they could be hunted and murdered," I replied coolie.

A few of his guys' eyes widened and they stared at Tino in disgust and horror. They clearly didn't realize what a sick fuck they worked for. Tino's eyes remained on me, unmoved by his men.

"I can't give you all the casinos. Only half," he informed me.

"Fine." I shrugged. He seemed relaxed by my words. "Then I'll only tell him about half the women."

"Come the fuck on!" He growled, slamming his fists on the table. My guys started to stand up, a few of them with their hands in their coat pockets no doubt gripping the handle of their guns. I signaled for them to stay in place, which they did obediently.

"As I said, this isn't much of a negotiation. You know the rules of the De Santos. You took the oath. No one to fucking blame but yourself." My finger pointed in his direction. "So either sign over the casinos or call your brother and De Santos and tell them what the fuck you did."

"You greedy son of a bitch!"

Before my guys could respond, I held up my hand and shook my head. A soft chuckle escaped me as I looked at the rage in Tino's eyes. A vein pulsated across his forehead. The fat fuck was ready to blow a gasket.

I had every intention of leaking the information to Tino's brother and De Santos once I got Tino to sign over the casinos *legally.* For now, I had to play the game of businessman. However, once the sick fuck was off my property, I'd be making a phone call or two.

"If that isn't calling the pot calling the kettle black, I don't know what it is," I sneered. "Tino, it's fucking simple. You sign over the casinos and that's that. Or you don't and you deal with your brother and De Santos. I'm sure they'll forgive you for sex trafficking and the murder and mutilation of fifty women. Right?"

The door to my office flew open, causing us all to startle.

"Fifty fucking women!" Sofia screamed as she stormed into the room.

"Sofia!" Tino gushed, standing up. He opened his arms to her but quickly raised his hands in a surrendering manner when he saw the gun pointed at him. "Sofia. Eh. Take it easy."

"Take it easy? Take it fucking easy?" she growled, continuing to aim the gun at him. "Fifty fucking women are dead because of you!"

"It– It– It isn't like that," he stammered. He looked at his guys and gestured with his eyes for one of them to do something to her.

"They're on my father's fucking payroll, mother fucker! If I want to blow your fucking head off, they'll help me dispose of your fucking body!" she shouted. "So don't fucking look at them for guidance. Capiche?"

Damn, she's fucking sexy, I thought looking her over.

"Sofia, you're blowing this way out of proportion."

"Sit. The. Fuck. Down," she growled, pointing at the seat with the gun. Tino staggered backward until his knees touched the seat.

"Sofia, let's just talk about this rationally," Tino said, sitting down with his eyes on her.

"Fucking explain. Now." Sofia paced a few feet from him but her eyes never left him. They were like lasers locked on their target. There was so much intensity coming from her.

The average person– man or woman– would be shaking as they held a gun to someone; not Sofia. She held it flawlessly as though it was another part of her body. Not a single shake, tremble, or hesitation as she aimed the gun at her uncle's head.

"I said explain," she gritted through clenched teeth.

"It was just business, Sofia," Tino replied. "I didn't hurt the women. I just supplied them."

"You piece of shit!" She charged over to him and without warning struck him in the head with the grip of the gun. Tino cried out in pain as he held his forehead where it was now split open. Bright red blood seeped from beneath his hands.

"You, bitch!" Tino shouted at her.

"Mind your fucking tone!" I growled, standing up and slamming my fists against the table. All eyes were on me. "Watch how you speak to her."

Out of the corner of my eye, I saw Sofia smirk.

Naughty little vixen, I chuckled to myself but kept myself calm on the outside.

"Wait outside," Sofia ordered with her eyes locked on Tino; however, her words weren't meant for him.

The tone in her voice and her facial expression were both as cold as ice. She was a woman out for blood. There'd be no stopping whatever she had planned for Tino.

My beautiful Sofia.

CHAPTER THIRTEEN

SOFIA

Antonio's guys looked at him for guidance. While the men who were with Tino looked at me. They knew at the end of the day, Tino had broken the Omerta Oath. His orders were no longer valid which now made me trump Tino and anything he said or did.

"Gabriele? Bosco? Lasciaci." I said, looking first at Gabriele then Bosco. They both stood behind Tino.

"Si, Signorina Sofia," Bosco replied, bowing his head. "Adiamo," he ordered the men under him.

"Where the fuck do you think you're going?" Tino spat.

The men ignored Tino's words. They bowed their heads at me in acknowledgment then walked out the door. Bosco stopped in the doorway. He looked at me.

"Signorina Sofia, we will be in the hallway, if you need us," Bosco said.

"Gratzi, Bosco," I replied with a smile. I had no anger towards him or any of the others. They clearly didn't know what my uncle had been up to. I could tell by the look on their faces. They were all disgusted.

There was a code to the mafia. A true mafia. You don't hurt women or children. Ever! And my uncle had blatantly broken that code by providing women to someone, knowing they'd be killed. If I didn't kill Tino, my father or Uberto De Santos himself would take his life.

The door closed quietly and Tino swallowed hard. He knew

he was truly alone. No one would come to his aid. No matter how much he screamed or begged, it would all fall on deaf ears.

I grabbed a chair and pulled it beside Tino. So much anger flowed through my blood as I stared at the fat slob. For so long I had held a grudge towards him; however, this was much more than a grudge. This was hate.

Out of the corner of my eye, I saw Antonio sit down and gesture to his guys. They sat down without hesitation. All of their attention was on Tino and me.

"How much?" I asked Tino calmly despite how bad I wanted to rip his head off.

"How much what?" Tino groaned.

"How much did he pay you for these women? In fact, who the fuck is *he*?" I looked at Antonio for that answer. "Who is the guy?"

"Manny Paloma," Antonio replied.

"Manny Paloma," I repeated softly. The name didn't sound familiar but I'd remember it for the rest of my life. "You know him?"

"Yes," Antonio nodded. "He worked for me."

Worked for him? Anger filled me. Why would he hire someone like that? It didn't make any sense. Antonio had been so kind to me. Was it an act? It didn't feel like an act. His touch, the look in his eyes. All of it felt real. There had to be more to this Manny Paloma.

I took a deep breath. Thoughts rushed through my mind as I tried to piece everything together. Then the lightbulb went off.

"You're extorting this fat fuck." I pointed at Tino but kept my eyes on Antonio, who grinned. "Aren't you? To get his businesses."

"Yes."

At least he was honest with me. I couldn't fault him for that.

"What's your plan after that?" I asked with an eyebrow raised.

"Hand him over to your father or De Santos."

"You piece of shit!" Tino growled. "You're going to hand me over after you get my hard-earned–"

"It's just business," Antonio chuckled, using Tino's own words against him.

"Yeah. It's just business, Uncle," I smiled sweetly at Tino. The look in his eyes as he stared at me screamed murder. If he had the chance, he'd kill all of us.

"I've worked hard to get where I am," Tino muttered.

"Worked hard? How is throwing around your brother's and De Santos' names count for you working hard? Lazy mother fucker. You mooch off of them. Carefully shaking their hand while your other hand is dipping into their pot behind their back."

Tino's eyes widened. I couldn't help the smirk that crossed my face. Antonio's words might surprised others; however not me. For a long time, I knew who my uncle truly was– A complete piece of shit.

"That's right. I've done my homework," Antonio grinned at Tino. "I know all about the *paid* protection you've offered people. Big-timers who think they're under the protection of the Romano and De Santos Families. But it's just your way to earn a dime. Right?"

"You– You– You don't know shit about me," Tino waved his finger at Antonio. "I was running these streets before you were even a thought in your daddy's– FUCK!"

Tino held his face. His eyes now locked on me. Intensity and rage filled them. I suppose striking him in the eye with the gun upset him. But he had it coming. I hadn't even thought twice about it. Simply, lifted the gun and with all my might hit him with it.

Stupid schmuck, I muttered to myself.

"Nonna raised you better." I tsked. "Such a Romano disgrace."

"You. Fucking. Bit–

Bang. The sound of a gun going off sounded throughout the room. Tino cried out in pain. Confusion filled me as I looked at the gun in my hand. How the fuck did I shoot Tino? My finger wasn't even on the trigger and the gun was on safe. What the hell happened?

Before I could digest the questions swarming my mind, Antonio stormed across the room and over to the other side of Tino, who was hunched over holding his shoulder. Antonio yanked Tino out of his chair forcefully. The chair crashed to the floor.

"I fucking told you to watch how you talked to her," Antonio gritted between clenched teeth inches from Tino's face. Tino shook with fear while his hand pressed firmly against his bullet wound.

"I– I– I–" Tino stuttered.

"Shut the fuck up!" Antonio growled. "Your breathing alone annoys the fuck out of me."

"You mother fucker," Tino muttered under his breath between ragged breaths.

"Tie him up downstairs." Antonio released his hold on Tino's shirt.

Tino stumbled backward into the wall. Before he had a chance to stand upright, two of Antonio's men snatched him up. Tino kicked and screamed as they dragged him towards the door.

"Wait," I said, walking over to behind them.

"Hold on," Antonio stated, causing the guys to stop walking. I quickly dug into Tino's front pocket and retrieved his phone.

"Okay. I'm good." I smiled. The guys nodded their heads then dragged Tino from the room. His loud, pathetic screams echoed throughout the hallway.

"Shut him up!" Antonio called out.

"You got it, Boss!" one of the men yelled, shortly before Tino's loudness fell silent.

"Leave us," Antonio ordered the room.

"Yes, Boss!" The remainder of my guys said in unison then filed out of the room.

"That was fun," I giggled, sitting down and spinning in the chair. "Are things always so lively around here?"

Antonio chuckled softly. He closed the door then walked over to me.

"You okay?" he asked, looking down at me.

"Of course. This is like a Tuesday in my house," I winked. Antonio laughed at my words. "Just saying."

Antonio helped me up then sat down. My eyebrow rose from his gesture but before I could open my mouth, he grabbed my hand. He pulled me onto his lap. My arms instinctively wrapped around his neck.

"Well, hello there," I laughed.

"Hello, Beautiful," he grinned. His finger strummed my hand that held the gun. "Where did you find a gun?"

His question made me laugh. Clearly, he knew nothing about me. I was a Romano.

"I'm a Romano, Antonio." He stirred at my use of his name. I sucked in a sharp breath as his hard-on pressed against my ass.

"A beautiful Romano. I might add," he smirked. My cheeks

warmed and I turned my head to hide it. "Don't know why you're so bashful about your looks."

"Anyway," I shook off my thoughts and faced him again. "The gun was in my carry-on. Your guys never searched my bags."

"Figures," he groaned. "Unacceptable."

I recognized the tone in his voice. He was furious with his guys for not doing a thorough job. If Antonio and I hadn't gotten along so… well, I could have killed him easily.

"Don't be so mad," I whispered. Softly, I pressed my lips against his. "It was an honest mistake. In their defense, most women don't carry weapons in their carry-ons."

"Kiss me again, and I'll think about letting them live," he smirked.

"Are you blackmailing me into saving them?" My eyebrow rose. I fought to keep from laughing. His childish antics were both amusing and flattering… in a sense.

"I mean, you can still kiss me and I'll handle them how I deem fit," he shrugged.

"But if I kiss you, they'll–"

My hand that held my uncle's cell phone vibrated. An annoying oldie song played loudly as the ringtone for the caller. My dad's image flashed across the screen.

"Who's he?" Antonio asked, pointing to the phone.

"That'd be the man himself."

"Your father?"

"Mmhmm."

"Going to answer?"

"Do you want me to?"

Antonio gestured for me to answer. Reluctantly, I pressed

talk on the call and held the phone up to my ear.

"Hello?" I answered.

"Sofia?" my father retorted in a questioning tone.

"Papa."

"Why the hell are you answering your uncle's phone?" he snapped. "And why are you ignoring my calls? I've been calling you since last night."

"Things got complicated. Did you talk to Uncle Tino last night?"

"I asked you a question, Sofia Romano." My father's tone was deep and filled with anger. I could picture the vein in his neck bulging. I'd be a liar if I said it didn't give me great satisfaction.

"Why are you smiling, Beautiful?" Antonio whispered into my ear. His warm breath caused a shiver to run up my spine. I bit back a moan and stared at him.

"Sofia Romano?" my dad roared into the phone. I pulled the phone away from my ear briefly then put it back up to my ear. My father was rambling on about how I never listened to him and how he was tired of being disrespected by everyone around him.

"Did you know Uncle Tino likes to have women imported into Las Vegas so they can be murdered?" I asked with a smug grin on my face.

"What! How dare you accuse your uncle of such a heinous crime, Sofia? He's your uncle. If you're mad that I made you go to Vegas, you can be mad at me but you don't accuse my brother of such a thing."

"This has nothing to do with me being upset with Uncle Tino, Papa. In fact, I didn't know until a friend told me what Uncle Tino was up to."

"A friend? Who is this friend?"

"Do you know Manny Paloma?"

"No," my father replied flatly. "Is that who is disgracing my brother's name?"

"Papa, I'm sorry. Uncle Tino admitted it to me. Do you consider me a liar?"

My father fell silent. I knew he was taking my words to heart. Our family lived by an oath. Loyalty and honesty were amongst that oath.

"No," he finally replied. "You are no liar."

"Thank you, Papa."

"Tell me what else you know about this."

"I know that he's taking money from people and telling them that they are now under the protection of the De Santos."

"What?" It was a hushed growl.

"Yes. He's been using De Santos' name to make money off people."

"Sofia, your friend told you all of this?"

"Yes."

"And you trust this… friend?"

I looked at Antonio. He stared at me with his piercing eyes. I melted like butter and realized just how hopeless I was.

"Yes. I trust my friend with every ounce of my being." Antonio smiled at my words then kissed me softly.

"I want to speak to your friend," my father sighed. "Give me his number."

"Papa, I have your word that no harm will come to my friend?"

Antonio rolled his eyes and chuckled.

I guess my question probably seemed silly considering Antonio was a mob boss. However, my father worked for one of the most ruthless mob bosses on the planet. If Antonio was going to talk to my father then I wanted a guarantee that no one would fuck with him. Ever.

"If he's no threat then he'll be safe," my father replied.

"No. I need a promise that he won't be touched."

"Sofia," my father warned. "Give me his number."

"I can't. Not until I know he'll be safe. I'll call you back in an hour." With that, I hung up the phone. I stared at Antonio with wide eyes. Horror washed over me.

"What's wrong?" Antonio asked, rubbing my back.

"I've– I've never done that before."

"Done what?"

"Hung up on my father... He's going to kill me," I blurted laughing.

CHAPTER FOURTEEN

ANTONIO

"I appreciate you trying to...um...protect me," I laughed. "However, I'm capable of holding my own so if you'd like, I'll talk to your father."

"No," Sofia shook her head. "I want his word first. Plus, you and I need to talk more before you speak with him."

"About?"

"He's going to want to know how we know each other. Then the floodgates will open from there," she sighed.

"Sofia?" I said, lifting her chin with my finger. When our eyes met, I smiled. "It'll be okay. I told you, I won't let anything bad come your way. You tell me what you want to tell your father and that's what I'll say."

"As simple as that?"

"As simple as that, Beautiful."

"Why are you so nice to me?" Her question made me frown.

"Why wouldn't I be nice to you?"

"I don't know. Just a question," she shrugged. She acted like none of it was a big deal but nervousness was written all over her face.

"Sofia," I kissed her gently then smiled. "I meant my words earlier. I'll do anything and everything to keep you safe."

Her cheeks reddened and she laid her head on my shoulder. I kissed the top of her head. My arms wrapped tighter around her, hoping she could feel the warmth and sincerity of my words.

"Is it crazy that I don't want to leave?" she whispered, causing my heart to skip several beats. Her question felt surreal.

"You don't?"

I was terrified of my question, but I needed to hear how she truly felt. Was I the only one falling hopelessly for a stranger? Or was life finally cutting me a break and Sofia felt the same way about me? Either way, I needed to know.

"No. I don't," she replied. She sat up and looked at me. "It's all like some sort of crazy-ass dream. Like how is it possible for me to feel like I've known you my entire life? And how come I'm not scared of you? A normal person would be fucking terrified of their captor; however, I've never felt safer."

The last of her words came out a hushed whisper, but they sounded off in my head like a cannon. The feelings that came over me could only be described with two words– true happiness.

"Going to say anything?" Sofia asked nervously.

"Sorry. Just taking it all in," I said, leaning my forehead against hers. "Your words have made me a very happy man, Sofia."

"What do we do now?"

"Whatever your heart desires, Beautiful."

"What do you want to happen?"

I pulled my head away from hers then looked down at her. I couldn't help the cheesy ass smile I had.

"I want you to be mine."

"In what sense?"

"Every sense, Sofia," I chuckled. It was my turn to be nervous. "I know we haven't even spent twenty-four hours together. I won't rush you into the decision I want you to make but I do want you to at least be my girlfriend and stay with me."

"Just like that? I'm your girlfriend and we live together?" I couldn't tell if she was making fun of my suggestion or if she was sincerely asking.

"Yes." I was too fucking scared to say anything else. The fear of scaring her off damn near brought me to my knees. I'd beg her to stay and be mine if I had to.

"What's this other decision you're talking about?"

A groan escaped me. Why did I put my foot in my mouth? She was really going to run for the hills if I answered her question honestly. But on the other hand, I refused to lie to her.

"It's greedy of me but I want you all to myself, Sofia. I don't want another man to get the opportunity to make you his," I took a deep breath. "I want you as my wife."

"Your wife?" she gasped.

And now she's going to fucking run for the hills.

"I know I sound like a fucking nutjob," I groaned. That's why I almost didn't say anything but when it comes to you, I can't help but tell the truth. You could ask me anything and I'd answer truthfully."

"Guess we're both fucking nutjobs," she giggled, making my eyebrow raise. "I would have said yes if you had asked me to marry you."

My entire world came to a screeching halt. I stared into Sofia's beautiful green eyes and searched for amusement or humor. I found none of those emotions in her look.

"You would have?" I asked dumbfoundedly.

"Mmhmm," she nodded. "I can't explain it. It's like all logic goes out the window when it comes to you."

"Is that a bad thing?" I grinned. She rolled her eyes and laughed.

"Not necessarily," she smiled and set the cell phone down on the table. She wrapped her arms around my neck. "There's just something about you, Antonio Berlusconi."

"And there's just something about you, Sofia Romano." I kissed the tip of her nose and smiled. "So... where does that leave us?"

"Depends."

"On?"

"If you're going to ask me out or not," Sofia grinned ear to ear.

Her boldness and no-fear attitude were some of the sexiest things about her. Usually, a woman wasn't a total package; however, not Sofia. She was super-model pretty, had a killer personality, and brains too.

The only problem was she was a Romano with connections to the De Santos Family. If her father didn't approve of Sofia and me being together, he could try to make my life hell by any means necessary; which could include De Santos getting involved. I was head of the Berlusconi Family– a mob boss – with my own army. If a war is what came to my door then I'd welcome it with guns blazing.

Fuck it, I thought as I kissed her passionately then pulled away slowly.

"You going to be my girl?" I asked grinning.

She laid her head on my shoulder and giggled, "Thought you'd never ask."

EPILOGUE

SOFIA

ONE MONTH LATER…

The wind on the tarmac was brutal. It was ice cold and whipped across my skin like razor blades. A shiver ran down my spine.

"I told you to wait on the plane, Babe," Antonio said, wrapping his arms around me tighter. "Let's get you back on board."

"No," I shook my head. "I want to see this through."

"Sofia," he chuckled and looked down at me. "You're just going to stay warm inside the plane and then come back out when they get here."

"You going to wait in there with me?" I asked with an eyebrow raised. He grinned then shook his head. "Exactly! So why the hell am I going to go back on the plane?"

"Because you're freezing that pretty little ass of yours off."

"Hush," I giggled and snuggled against his chest.

"Babe, I don't like you out here. It's too windy," he whispered tenderly.

Typical Antonio. Always being considerate of my feelings and an absolute gentleman.

The past month had been like a dream come true. If someone had asked me a few weeks ago, if I'd ever move in with a guy who had kidnapped me, I would have yelled *HELL NO!* But look at me now. I was living my best life with a man, who made me beyond happy.

"What are you thinking about, Beautiful?" Antonio asked softly. I looked up to find him staring down at me with concern sketched on his face.

"Just thinking about how we met and how things have been going these past few weeks," I admitted.

"And? Is this good or bad?"

"Definitely good. Duh?" I stuck out my tongue, making him laugh. "For the first time in my life, I feel my true self and absolutely happy."

Antonio smiled wide then dipped his head and kissed me passionately. He kissed me as though there was no tomorrow. I moaned against his lips and clung to his jacket when my knees weakened from emotions.

Antonio slowly broke our kiss.

"You deserve to be happy, Sofia," he smiled. "Always."

"Are you happy?" I asked, looking up at him with hopeful eyes.

"Absolutely."

"Good. That makes me– They're here!" I interrupted myself when I saw an entourage of black SUVs heading down the tarmac towards us. Nerves instantly filled me.

My father had wanted both Antonio and my Uncle Tino's head. He wanted Antonio dead because he kidnapped me. My dad wanted Tino's head because Tino was responsible for the death of so many women and had used Romano and De Santos' names in vain.

The past four weeks, I had spent countless hours negotiating with my father. My terms were simple: I'd give him Tino and no harm would come to Antonio. However, my father retorted with how Antonio needed to know his place and be made an example of for kidnapping me. Each time, I'd snap on my dad then hang up the phone.

Antonio assured me that everything would work out. He even went as far as to say that he'd fly to New Jersey to speak to my father face-to-face. That would be a suicide mission.

Crazy fucker, I thought, glancing up at Antonio.

My father and I finally came to an agreement, against both our dismay. The agreement was Antonio and I would fly to New Jersey to hand over my uncle directly to my father. At this time, my father would decide if he forgave Antonio for his actions towards our family and me.

"Breathe, Babe," Antonio whispered into my ear.

"You should have let me bring my fucking gun," I growled, making him laugh.

"You can't shoot your dad, Sofia."

"Wanna bet?" I sassed, waving my finger in his face. "If he even thinks about harming a hair on your head, I'll kill him with my bare fucking hands. I swear I will!"

"You're so sexy when you're mad," Antonio smirked.

"Hush." I turned my head so he couldn't see me smile.

"Mmhmm. I saw that," he chuckled. "Showtime."

The SUVs stopped a few feet from us. My stomach knotted. It was unsettling not having a gun to ensure that my father behaved. I wasn't sure what I'd do if my father killed Antonio.

Several doors opened and people filed out of the cars. They were my dad's goons. They were armed with machine guns. The hairs on the back of my neck stood.

"Relax, Sofia," Antonio said softly. "He's just trying to intimidate me. I'm not scared."

"If he... If he hurts you–" I choked on my own words as I

tried to hold back tears.

"Babe, it's fine," he assured me, kissing the top of my head.

Antonio did a hand signal, in the direction of the plane. The door to the plane opened and two of Antonio's men walked down the stairs with Uncle Tino. My uncle wore a black bag over his head and his hands were zip-tied in front of him.

They bounded down the stairs and over to us. There was a movement near one of the SUVs. A passenger door opened. The entire vibe around me intensified and I held my breath.

It'll be okay. It'll be okay, I repeated to myself over and over.

"Sofia, breathe." Antonio kissed the side of my head. I didn't trust myself to speak. I was scared out of my mind to see my father. What if–

"Oh, my God!" I squealed and took off over to the SUV. My arms wrapped around Adrianna.

"You act like we haven't seen each other in years," she giggled, hugging me back.

"I'm so fucking happy to see you!" I said a little too excitedly.

"I'm happy to see you too," Adrianna laughed but stopped abruptly. She glared behind me. "Is that him?"

"Uncle Tino?" I asked, turning to look at Antonio, my uncle, and Antonio's men.

"No! The fucker who fucking kidnapped you, Sofia! What the fuck!" she snapped at me. "I mean, what the– Wait? Is that the hottie from the wedding?"

Her words made me giggle.

"Yes. That's the *hottie* from the wedding," I replied.

"How the hell did that happen?" Adrianna asked with her arms crossed in front of her chest and an eyebrow raised.

"I'll explain, but first, where's Dad?"

"He sends his regards," she grinned ear-to-ear.

"What!" I gasped in disbelief. He wasn't coming?

"Let me get this fucking dickhead uncle of ours and then I'll give you his message okay?"

"Okay."

We walked over to Antonio and them with my dad's goons flanking us. Adrianna stood in front of our uncle but looked at Antonio.

"Hello again," she smirked.

"Miss Romano," Antonio said coolie, grinning.

"Adrianna? Adrianna? Is that you?" my uncle gasped. "Tell these fuckers to let me go! Tell them–"

Tino's words were cut off with Adrianna's knee to his balls. He dropped to the ground in pain.

"You fucking bitch!" Tino spat. Adrianna grabbed his head and kneed him forcefully in the face. I heard bones crack from the blow. Tino cried out.

I couldn't see his face but there was no doubt that he was covered in bed. His nose was most likely off-set from now being broken.

"Take him to the car," Adrianna ordered, snapping her fingers. One of my father's men yanked Tino up by his bound hands.

"No! No! Please, stop!" Tino blubbered as he was dragged off to one of the SUVs, kicking and screaming.

"Leave us," Antonio instructed his guys. Again, just like obedient servants they left without protest and went back onto the plane.

"Go back to the car," Adrianna said. My father's men exchanged looks with one another. They weren't as compliant as Antonio's men. "I want to talk to my sister and him. I won't ask again."

"As you wish, Signorina Romano," one of them replied. He gestured for them to all load up, which they did within seconds, leaving Adrianna alone with Antonio and me.

"If you hurt her, I'll kill you," Adrianna said suddenly. I groaned at her threat while Antonio nodded. "If you make her cry, I'll kill you. If you make her unhappy, I'll kill you. You cheat on her, I'll cut off your dick and feed it to you."

"Adrianna!" I growled.

"It's okay, Sofia," Antonio whispered. "I don't plan on doing any of that so I'm safe." The last of his words was a chuckle.

"I mean it," Adrianna assured him.

"I'll hold you to it," he retorted. Surprisingly, Adrianna laughed then pulled me into her arms.

"Looks like you're in good hands, Sofia. So I'm going to head back to the house. I'm in charge of handling our uncle."

"Just like that?" I asked in disbelief.

This all seemed way too easy. My father hadn't shown up, Adrianna accepted Antonio's answer, and this was all over now. None of that added up.

"Yep. That's what Papa ordered," she replied, letting go of me. She shrugged her shoulders and turned towards the SUVs.

"You're going to leave?"

"I'm being tested so I have to head back to the house." My eyebrow rose as I took in her words. "I'm next in line for head of the Romano Family."

Her words would have surprised anyone, but not me.

Adrianna was the oldest of us girls. She was ruthless, cut-throat, obedient, and a force to be reckoned with. Her being the head of our family made sense. Others would have a problem with it since she was *a girl*; however, they'd learn to respect *HER.* Or they'd feel her wrath.

"I'm so happy for you, Adrianna," I smiled.

"Yeah. Yeah. Don't go getting sappy on me. I still have a long time before Papa steps down," she replied, shaking her head and walking off.

"Hey! What was his message?"

Adrianna glanced back over her shoulder and grinned mischievously.

"He said, *Tell my little girl I'm proud of the woman she's become. She's a true Romano standing her ground,*" she smiled brightly. "You made the bastard proud, Sofia. See you later!" She threw up a peace sign then got back into the car she had gotten out of. They drove off into the night, leaving Antonio and me standing alone.

"See, it all worked out," Antonio said, pulling me into his arms. Wrapping me in his warmth and love.

"That all seemed so…" My words drifted off.

"Surreal?"

"Yes. That's a good word for all of this," I giggled and hugged him. "I feel so fucking relieved right now."

"Good." He kissed the top of my head and held one of my hands. "Let's go home."

The thought of us going back to Vegas made me smile. It was the last place on Earth I ever thought I'd call home; however, it had become just that– home.

"Sounds good," I stood on my tippy toes and kissed him softly. "Let's go home."

THE END

SISTER BOOKS

Sofia: Vanished Series: *Vanished in Vegas* by S.E. Isaac (February 2022)

Rosaline: Flower of the Month Series: *The Hitman's Rose* by S.E. Isaac (June 2022)

Adrianna: *The Made Daughter* by S.E. Isaac (May 2022)